A Mango-Shaped Space

wendy mass

LB
Little, Brown and Company
New York Boston

Also by Wendy Mass:
Jeremy Fink and the Meaning of Life
Leap Day
Heaven Looks a Lot Like the Mall
Every Soul a Star
The Candymakers

Little, Brown and Company

Hachette Book Group
237 Park Avenue, New York, NY 10017
Visit our website at www.lb-kids.com

Little, Brown and Company is a division of Hachette Book Group, Inc.
The Little, Brown name and logo are trademarks of Hachette Book Group, Inc.

First Revised Edition: November 2010
First published in hardcover in April 2003 by Little, Brown and Company

ISBN 978-0-316-52388-2 (hc) / ISBN 978-0-316-05825-4 (pb)
LCCN 2002072989

15 14 13 12 11

Printed in the United States of America

The text was set in Janson Text, and the display type is Providence Sans.

For Joseph, who is new
For my grandparents, who are not
And in memory of Merlin

Freak. FREEEEEEK.

I'll never forget the first time I heard the word, that day at the blackboard. It was five years ago, when I was eight. (For those who are mathematically challenged, like me, that means I'm thirteen now.) So there I was, dressed in my shepherd-girl costume for the Christmas play after school, struggling to complete the math problem on the board while my fellow third-graders watched. The one-size-fits-all costume didn't fit me, the shortest shepherd in the class, so I had to keep pushing up the sleeves. The chalk dust tickled my nose. My feet were freezing in the sandals that in my humble opinion no one should have to wear in northern Illinois in the middle of December. My mission was to multiply twenty-four times nine. I remember thinking that if I wrote slowly enough, the bell might ring before I could finish. Just five more minutes. Then no one would know that I couldn't solve the problem.

I rolled the smooth piece of chalk around my fingers and tried not to think about the whole class staring at my back. Glancing around in what I hoped looked like intense concentration, I noticed a few fragments of colored chalk on the ledge of the board. To use up some time, I put down the white piece and began rewriting each number on the board in its correct color.

"Mia!"

My teacher, Mrs. Lowe, startled me. As I turned, the chalk screeched on the board and a deep-red zig-zag shape sped across my field of vision. My classmates groaned at the noise. "This isn't art class," she said, wagging her long, skinny finger at me as if I didn't know that. "Just use the white chalk."

"But isn't it better to use the right colors?" I asked, confident that the other kids would agree.

The class giggled and I grinned, thinking they were laughing at her, not me.

"What do you mean, the right colors?" she asked, sounding genuinely confused and more than a little annoyed. Now *I* became confused. Wasn't it obvious what I meant? I looked at my classmates for help, but now their expressions had changed. They gawked at me as if I had suddenly sprouted another head. My hands started to shake a little, and I rushed out my explanation.

"The colors. The colors of the numbers, you know,

like the two is pink, well of course it's not really *this* shade of pink, more like cotton-candy pink, and the four is this baby-blanket blue color, and I...I just figured it would be easier to do the math problem with the numbers in the correct colors. Right?" I pleaded with my classmates—my friends—to back me up.

This time when the class laughed it didn't sound so friendly. I felt my cheeks burning. Then I heard it. In a loud whisper from the back row. *Freak*. Except it sounded like *FREEEEK*.

"What are you talking about, Mia?" demanded my now clearly irate teacher. "Numbers don't have *colors*, they simply have a shape and a numerical value, that's all."

"But they have all those things," I whispered, my voice sounding far away.

Mrs. Lowe put her hands on her hips. "I've had enough of this. For the last time, numbers do not have colors. Now, are you going to complete the assignment?"

I stared at her and shook my head. I suddenly felt very small, as if my skin was tightening and I was actually shrinking. A whirring sound filled my head. How was this possible? Was everyone playing a trick on me? Of course numbers had colors. Were they also going to tell me that letters and sounds didn't have colors?

That the letter *a* wasn't yellow like a faded sunflower and screeching chalk didn't make red jagged lines in the air? I replaced the chalk on the ledge, aware for the first time that my hands shake when I'm nervous. I stood with my arms at my sides, sleeves hanging half-way to my knees. Was I the only one who lived in a world full of color? I waited to see if they were going to tell me the earth was flat.

A badly constructed paper airplane wobbled past my nose.

Mrs. Lowe sent me to Principal Dubner's office, where I repeated my explanation for using the colored chalk. By the time my parents arrived an hour later, I'd run out of steam. I sat there and listened to them talk about my "uncharacteristic behavior." I wanted to tell the principal that his name was the color of freshly piled hay. I quickly thought better of it. Even at eight years old, I was smart enough to realize that some-thing was very wrong and that until I figured out what it was, I'd better not get myself in deeper trouble.

So I pretended I made everything up. I sat there and said things like "It was stupid," "I was only playing around." And, at least twenty times, "I'm sorry."

The principal left me in the hands of my parents, who brought me home. I promptly kicked off the stu-pid sandals, threw on my sneakers, and took off running through the fields behind my house. The cold didn't bother me. I was too busy brooding over the unfairness of it all.

The Christmas play was short one shepherd girl.

Mrs. Lowe made me clean the erasers for a week and apologize in front of the whole class for taking up their time with my nonsense. Those were her words, not mine.

Pretty soon, everyone forgot about that day. Everyone but me. I learned to guard my secret well. But now I'm thirteen. Everything is about to change.

And there's nothing I can do to stop it.

Chapter One

"A *is for Amy who fell down the stairs,*" says my best friend, Jenna Davis, as we climb farther down into the steep, parched ravine. We've been inseparable since we were five and her mother brought her to my house to play. We bonded over the various ways we could contort my Barbie and Ken dolls without breaking them. Let's just say that Ken won't be having children anytime soon and leave it at that.

"B *is for Basil, assaulted by bears,*" I reply, continuing the morbid rhyme we memorized off the poster on my bedroom wall. Each letter of the alphabet has a rhyme about a little kid meeting some bizarre end. I like the poster because it is in black and white to everyone else, but inside my head, it's in color.

"Could it be any hotter out?" Jenna asks, panting with the effort to keep her footing on the slippery slope.

The sweat dripping down my face is enough of an answer. August has rolled around too soon, and we only have a few more weeks before eighth grade starts.

If we lived a little farther south, a tumbleweed would tumble by. As we stumble down the familiar path of tall, sun-bleached grass and dry earth, I can feel the air thickening, preparing for a storm.

At thirteen, Jenna and I are much too old for day camp. We already live out in the country, with all the fresh air we could want. We entertain ourselves by pretending there is still some square inch of country-side that we haven't discovered yet. Every day we explore the hills, the valley in between, the ravine, the woods. Last summer we found an arrowhead half buried under a bush. My father said it might have been from the Blackhawk War, the one that Abe Lincoln fought in when he was young. This year all we've found is the same old crabgrass, same old bugs, same old us. But still, exploring passes the time. The absence of wind today means we're spared the smell of manure from the Roth's farm across the valley. That's something to be thankful for.

When we were younger, we used to pretend that the ravine, always dry like this during the summer months, would lead us someplace else—somewhere magical, with adventures and swords and talking animals like in the Narnia books. Sometimes I still catch Jenna peeking behind bushes for hidden doorways. She's trying to find a way to reach her mother, who died three years ago from some kind of cancer that only women get. Mrs. Davis was so sweet and pretty, with red hair and freckles just like Jenna. Except Jenna is short like me, and Mrs. Davis was really tall. Before she died, Jenna's mom bought us the rope friendship bracelets that we have never taken off. She said that as long as we kept them on, nothing could come between us. I explain this to my own mother every time she begs me to cut off the bracelet, which is now too tight to slip over my hand. Who cares if it's gray and fraying and maybe even a little smelly?

The wind starts up slightly, and a big green leaf sticks to the sweat on my leg. I hold still and count to twelve before it flutters and falls to the ground. The color of the leaf is exactly the same color as Jenna's name—a bright, shimmering shade of green with some yellow highlights. I think part of why I liked Jenna right away is that I like the color of her name. But I'd never tell her that, nor would I tell my older sister, Beth, that her name is the murky brown of swamp water. Beth is sixteen and in the process of wearing down our parents' patience. She changes her hair color the way normal people change their under-wear. We used to be a lot closer, before she went to high school and dropped me like a piping-hot bag of microwave popcorn. Before she left for the summer, she told me the boys would pay more attention to me if I colored my hair blond. I told her I'd stick with my boring brown, thank you very much. The only natural blond in the family is Zack. He just turned eleven, and his name is the light blue of a robin's egg. Zack has a lot of strange ideas. He can tell you exactly how many McDonald's hamburgers he's eaten in his lifetime. He has a detailed chart on his wall. The local paper ran a story about it once.

Jenna stops walking and points at my feet. "Your sneakers are untied," she says. "For a change."

I kick my sneakers off, tie the laces together, and drape them over my shoulder. I prefer to be barefoot anyway. Every night, the water in the bottom of my shower turns brown for a minute as the dirt runs from between my toes. Beth refuses to shower after me.

Jenna starts to say something, but her words get drowned out by a helicopter flying overhead. The roaring sound instantly fills my vision with brown streaks and slashes, and I look up to see the familiar markings of my father's chopper. He sells and repairs small farm equipment and uses the helicopter to get to out-of-the-way places. Jenna and I wave, long hair whipping around our faces, but I don't think he sees us. When Zack was little, he was scared Dad wouldn't be able to find his way home. Zack cried and cried every time the helicopter took off. Finally Dad took me and Beth and Zack up in the chopper with him to show us how easy it is to spot the landing site. Beth threw up the entire time and hasn't gone for a ride since.

"Are you ever scared to fly with him?" Jenna asks when we can hear each other again. "That thing looks like it's ready to fall apart."

"It's fun," I tell her, tucking my hair back in its ponytail. "It feels like you're a bird up there. Everything looks different. You're always welcome to come with us, you know."

A look of horror flits across Jenna's face. "No thanks."

In all these years, Jenna has never accepted my offer.

"So have you gone up to the cemetery yet?" she asks as we continue walking along the bottom of the ravine.

"No, not yet. I still have to finish the painting." It was Jenna's idea that I bring my grandfather a present on the one-year anniversary of his death. She brings her mother something each year, and her mother gives her gifts from the grave. Well, sort of. When Mrs. Davis knew she wasn't going to live much longer, she stocked up on presents and wrote long letters about her life. She gave them to my mother to keep, and each year on Jenna's birthday, my mother sends her one of the packages in the mail. One of these years, the gifts are going to run out and that will be a very sad birthday indeed.

"Can I see the painting?" Jenna asks, even though she knows better.

"You know it's bad luck to show it before it's done."

"Why are you so superstitious?" she asks, wiping her sweaty brow and leaving a streak of dirt. "I thought your brother's superstitions drove you crazy."

"They do," I insist. "I'm not half as bad as him. If a black cat crosses his path, he locks himself in his room for the rest of the day. And forget walking under ladders. If he sees our father do it, he makes him walk around the house backward. *Twice.* Zack says that if Dad really wanted to make sure he undid the bad luck, he would cross his fingers until he saw a dog."

"But you don't have a dog."

"I know."

"And what's with the ladder thing anyway?"

I shrug. "I have no idea. But you definitely don't want to walk under one."

"There's a lot of weirdness in your family," Jenna says, picking at a scab on her elbow.

She doesn't even know about my own personal

brand of weirdness. Like everybody else, she seems to have forgotten about my third-grade incident. Which is just fine with me.

"You know," Jenna says, stepping carefully over a gnarled branch, "my father told me it could take a soul a whole year to reach heaven. Maybe that's why it took you a year to finish the painting of your grandfather."

I have my own theory on my grandfather's soul, but I haven't told anyone. After all, I am good at keeping secrets. "That could be it," I respond. "C'mon, let's get back so it doesn't take me any longer. I want to bring the painting to the cemetery before dinner."

"Do we have time for a quick PIC mission?" Jenna asks as we climb back up the slope.

I hated to skip out on the best part of the day, our PIC mission. Partners in Crime. The term was another gift from Jenna's mom. She made it up after she caught me standing guard while Jenna stole quarters from the cow-shaped cookie jar in their kitchen. After that we learned to be more careful. In fifth grade, we hid in Beth's closet when she had a slumber party. We heard lots of juicy gossip, as well as some stuff about how babies are made that cleared up a few lingering questions. To this day, Jenna and I count that as our most successful mission.

"I really can't today," I tell her.

"Oh, it's okay. I can't think of anything good anyway. This town is just too boring." She kicks up a pile of dirt with the toe of her sneaker and sighs loudly.

It takes longer than it should to get home because we have to walk all the way around the Davises' fields. Jenna's father actually farms his land; he grows soybeans and the sweetest corn for miles around. My father plowed under our fields to make the landing space for his helicopter. Jenna's father thinks my father is lazy since he only flies three times a week and is back by dinnertime. My father thinks Jenna's father should mind his own business.

"Is your dad ever going to stop working on your house?" Jenna asks as we come into view of it. Everyone in town, including the rest of my family, wants to know the answer to that question. The helicopter is now parked out back, and my father is already halfway up the ladder on his way to the roof.

"I don't think so," I reply honestly.

My sprawling house is famous in these parts and never fails to get a reaction. First, people stare. They look up; they look down. Sometimes they even do that twice. The house is almost like a living creature that keeps expanding and contracting and remaking itself. Every inch of it was built by my father and grandfather from all different kinds of wood—whatever they could borrow, barter, or beg for. They could never agree on how the house should be laid out, so they each did their own thing and eventually met up in the middle.

This technique resulted in a number of doors that lead nowhere and stairs that go inside walls like secret passageways. That is how Jenna and I managed to wind up in the back of Beth's closet, so I guess the spider web–filled tunnels are good for something. My father is usually on a ladder hammering away at the roof when he's not tinkering with the chopper. I call him Casper because we hardly ever see him at ground level. He calls me Wild Child because I'm always running around barefoot feeling the earth under my feet and predicting rain.

"Hi, Mr. Winchell," Jenna shouts.

My father waves at us with his hammer, his mouth full of nails.

"Bye, Mr. Winchell," Jenna shouts again as she heads toward her own smaller and much more normal house.

He tries to wave again, slips slightly, then quickly regains his balance.

"How long will you be up there?" I call out.

"Till your mother makes me come down."

"Great," I mutter. That means at least a few more hours of hammering until Mom brings Beth back from the airport. Beth's been gone for six whole weeks at a summer college-prep program in California. She won a full scholarship by writing an essay on the pressure of writing an essay. It was Zack's idea. Her return is all too soon if you ask me. It was nice not having anyone boss me around.

The hammering begins and the familiar mottled gray bursts of color appear about a foot away from my face. The color and shape of a hammer hitting a nail has become such a part of my existence that I barely notice it. I can see right through the color-bursts, but they still distract me from whatever I'm doing. If it was a nicer color, I might not mind as much.

I slip into my sneakers as I approach the back kitchen door, stepping cautiously around wooden planks, hammers, nails, and one very scary-looking chain saw. As always, the smell of sawdust is in the air and on my clothes and in my throat. It is inescapable around here, and it has long since mingled with the taste of multicolored chalk dust that still haunts me from third grade.

I go up to my room and look for Mango, whose official name is Mango the Magnificat. He usually sleeps at the foot of my bed on my old Winnie-the-Pooh baby blanket, completely covering the faded Pooh and Piglet walking into the sunset. He's not there now, but he left behind his favorite toy—a stuffed Tweety Bird that he likes to carry around in his mouth. I call out his name and hear a faraway, orange-soda-colored meow in response. I trace the sound to Beth's room and find the little gray-and-white traitor curled up on Beth's pillow. I swoop him up in my arms and glance at Beth's night table. By some huge oversight on her part, Beth left her diary right out in plain sight when she went to California. When I first noticed it, I thought maybe she *wanted* me to read it. Then I decided that she had probably booby-trapped it somehow and she'd know if I peeked.

I deposit Mango on my blanket, where he belongs. I start to shut the door behind me, when Zack sticks his foot in the way.

"Just a sec, Mia," Zack says, pushing the door back open. "I need to do something."

"You need to do something in my room?" I ask, instantly suspicious. Zack has only recently gotten over his destructive phase. For years, nothing in the house was safe. He was very good at taking things apart but much less skilled at the art of putting them back together.

"Don't worry," he insists. "It will only take a second."

"On one condition," I say, trapping him in the

doorway. "You have to tell me why it's bad luck to walk under a ladder."

He rolls his eyes. "That's easy. It's because you're disrupting the sacred triangle of life formed by the ladder, the ground, and the wall."

"Huh?" I let my guard down, and he takes this opportunity to brush past me into my room. He heads directly over to my clock collection on the far wall. I follow him and notice he's clutching several watches in his small hands. Two belong to my father, one is my mother's, and one is Beth's.

"What are you doing with all those wa—"

"Shh," he says, cutting me off. "I have to get this exactly right." He stares at the faces of my clocks as if they have a message for him.

"Get *what* exactly ri—"

"Shh!" His eyes dart from the wooden cuckoo clock to the fluorescent star-shaped one, over to the big digital one, down to the clock in the shape of a train, and across to the electronic one that speaks the time out loud. I've collected clocks since first grade. Every Christmas, I get to pick out another one.

"I have to set these watches exactly right," Zack explains, busily twisting the watch dials to match the time on my synchronized clocks. "Otherwise, some of us will be living in the past and some in the future. In the very same house! Can't have that. Very bad."

"What difference could a minute or two make?"

"It has to do with folds in the space-time continuum, obviously," he replies, as though I should clearly have known that.

"Where did you get that from? It sounds like something from *Star Trek*."

He shakes his head adamantly. "I read it on the NASA Web site."

I should have known. Zack is addicted to the Internet. "You can't believe everything you read on the comput—"

I don't get to finish my sentence because at that moment all the clocks strike five. The cuckoo pops out and cuckoos. Loudly. The train blows its whistle. *Really* loudly. All the alarms go off at the same time—buzzing and chiming and ringing and shrieking—all much louder than I've ever heard them. My father is still hammering. My mother honks in the driveway to let us know she is back from the airport with Beth. Beth slams the front door open and drops her suitcase on the floor. Mango runs under the bed. I put my hands over my ears and shut my eyes to stop all the colors that are bombarding me.

It doesn't work. My sight is filled with blurry purple triangles and waves of green and floating black dots and balls of all sizes and shades of colors, spinning, swooping, swirling in front of me and across the room and in my mind's eye. If I had been prepared, I would have been able to anticipate the onslaught, but now it is overwhelming and I feel like I'm suffocating.

"What's wrong with you?" Zack shouts. I'm crouching on the floor now.

"Why is everything so loud?" I cry above the noise.

A second later the chimes stop. No more honking, no more doors slamming, just the usual hammering. The colors and shapes quickly fade away, and I feel like I can breathe again. I open my eyes to find Zack staring at me with a combination of concern and surprise. I stand up and quickly turn one of the clocks around. The volume was turned all the way up. The same with the others. My hand shakes slightly as I pull them all off the wall and rest them on the bed.

"I don't get it. I always keep the alarms turned off."

Zack tries to slink out of the room, but I grab his sleeve. I hold him there until he confesses.

"Okay, I switched on the alarms and turned the volume up a little before you came home. I did it so I'd be able to hear them from my room."

"You could have heard them from your room if your room was in Alaska!" I push him into the hall and lock my door.

"Hey," he says, knocking hard. "I only did it so I wouldn't be in your room without permission."

"You were in here without permission to turn the alarms on, weren't you?"

Silence. Then, "What's your problem anyway?"

Ignoring him, I switch off the alarms and hang the clocks in their rightful spots. I watch them silently ticking and blink back the stinging tears. How could Zack be so unaffected by the noise? What if I'd been out in public when something like that happened? I'd look pretty ridiculous crouching in the hallway at school.

As I stand there feeling sorry for myself, Mango peeks out from his hiding place, looks around, then tentatively crawls out and winds himself around my legs. I pick him up and head over to the closet, where I store my art supplies. I have a painting to finish and a grandfather to visit. I always put music on when I paint, but for the first time I can remember, I'm afraid that the colors will overwhelm me. I never want to feel so out of control again.

I try to finish the painting, but I can't concentrate. It's too quiet. Even the hammering has stopped. I choose a Mozart piece that Grandpa used to like, turn the volume way down, and press the Play button before I can chicken out. The colors immediately and gently flow over me, energizing me, reminding me that I can still enjoy them. The glossy red-barnlike color of the violin, the silvery-bluish white of the flute, the school-bus yellow of the French horn. All of them layering on top of one another, changing, shifting, belonging, at that minute, only to me.

Chapter Two

I stand back to admire my work. Against a background of blue-gray sky, my grandfather seems to gaze right at me. His round face has the look of someone waiting for something that has been a long time coming.

But something is still missing. Staring at the painting, I finally realize what it is. I wash off my brush and prepare the gray and white paints. Brush stroke by brush stroke, Mango appears, perched on Grandpa's right shoulder. I can only fit a kitten-size Mango in the small space. I stand back and study it, pleased with the result. After a whole year, the painting is now finished. Mango fits on Grandpa's shoulder like the last piece of a puzzle. It makes perfect sense, considering where I first found Mango.

I can hear Mango wheeze from across the room as I pack up my watercolors. He was wheezing that first day too, the little yellow-orange puffs of air wafting around him. It was the day of Grandpa's funeral. The whole family was standing around the grave, crying and holding hands, offering Grandpa up to heaven.

Living in the country, we're used to offering small animals up to heaven, but then it's usually only Zack who's crying over the skunk or possum. This was totally different. The local minister—who I'd only met once before—was in the middle of his closing prayer when I glanced over and saw a tiny kitten. He was sitting about three feet away from the grave, and he had Grandpa's eyes—round and kind and all-knowing. I loved him immediately.

It took two weeks of relentless begging before my parents agreed to lift their "no animals in the house" rule. Everyone thinks I named him Mango because of his orange eyes, but that's not the case. I named him Mango because the sounds of his purrs and his wheezes and his meows are all various shades of yellow-orange, like a mango in different seasons.

We had to bring him to the vet right away because of the wheeze. Mango threw up twice during the twenty-minute ride, and my mother was not happy. The vet told us that Mango was born with a deep rip in the lining of one lung and that it couldn't be fixed. She said that if he lived another month, his body would probably compensate for it and he'd be okay.

That was a year ago. Mango still has the wheeze, but I still have Mango.

I should probably go downstairs and say hello to Beth.

But I really want to go up to the cemetery to give Grandpa his present before dinner. I gently lift the painting off the easel and almost drop it when my father knocks on my door. I steady the painting and unlock the door.

"We're going to take Beth to the drugstore," he says, wiping his dirt-covered hands on his faded jeans. "Do you want to come?"

"I have to clean all this up," I tell him, gesturing over my shoulder toward the easel and paints. For some reason I don't want to tell him that the picture is a gift for Grandpa. He hasn't mentioned what today is, and I don't want to remind him.

"Can I see it?" He walks in and studies the painting intently.

"This is really something." He sounds genuine, but it's hard to tell with parents. "You have a great sense of color."

If only he knew the half of it! "Thanks," I reply.

"They say the eyes are the windows to the soul, you know. I can see Grandpa in those eyes." My father knows important things, even if he isn't "book smart" like my mother, who was a high school science teacher until Zack was born.

"It's interesting how you did this," he says, peering more closely at the painting. "You made Mango's and Grandpa's eyes the same shape."

I smile to myself, pleased that he noticed. Just then, Beth yells up from downstairs, and my father pats me on the head as if I'm a child and turns to go.

"It's gonna rain," I warn him as he heads down the long hall, Mango at his heels.

He laughs and says there isn't a cloud in the sky. But I hear him tell Beth to take an umbrella.

As soon as the front door slams shut, I grab the canvas, pull on my sneakers, and run out the back. Grandpa is buried in the small cemetery on the hill about a half-mile past our house, snuggled right up next to Grams, who died when I was three. They are my dad's parents, but my mother was very close to them. Her own parents are still alive in Florida, but we don't see them because they won't fly. I think there's more to the story, something to do with "marrying beneath one's station" and the "dearth of culture in farm country," whatever that means. Mom never talks about it.

Jenna's mother is buried in the same cemetery, and I intend to stop by and pay my respects. I'm halfway to the cemetery with the still partially wet portrait held carefully away from my body when I notice Mango is following me. I wait for him to catch up, but he keeps getting distracted. There are a lot of things out here to catch a cat's attention. The fields back up to acres of overgrown land, complete with a thriving ecosystem of creepy crawling things, various small animals, and, according to tales Grandpa used to tell, the souls of the dead who once farmed this land.

Once, Grandpa led Zack and me through the woods until we came across a huge piece of green foam that was half buried in the thick brush. Zack, who was only six at the time, announced that it was a piece of the moon that had fallen to Earth. Grandpa said surely that's what it was, and he ripped off a chunk of it. I knew the foam was the inside of some rotting old couch cushion, but I played along. Grandpa made a little speech over that piece of cushion, holding it in front of him as if it were some priceless jewel. "As your guide on this trail," he said, his voice deep and reverent, "it is my honor to hereby bestow upon you both a little piece of the moon." He tore the chunk in half and handed each of us a piece about the size of an egg. It was squishy and moist, and the green color rubbed off on my fingers. I put it in a little box and hid it safely in the back of my desk drawer. I have no idea what Zack did with his.

I know Grandpa's soul isn't wandering the woods like the ghosts I sometimes think I glimpse between the trees. Part of his soul is right next to me, stored safe and sound inside Mango. I knew this as soon as I saw the little kitten sitting by Grandpa's grave that day, looking up at me with Grandpa's eyes. I firmly believe that people's souls can splinter off when they die. Part of Grandpa is inside of Mango, part is in heaven dancing with Grams (who was a really good dancer), and only Grandpa himself knows where the rest of him is. This is just my own personal theory.

As we rise over the last ridge, I can see Grandpa's grave clearly because the grass covering it is shorter than the rest. The headstones are glowing with the last of the sun, and I see a glint of something shiny resting on Grandpa's. When I reach it, I discover it's a bottle of my grandfather's favorite brand of beer. Dad must have left it there along with the flowers on Grams's headstone. I know he misses them a lot, even though he always says, "When it's your time to go, it's your time to go." God's will and all that. We're not a very religious family, but where death is concerned, it pays to be open-minded. I try not to think about death too much. I'm not good with endings. They make me too sad.

"Hi, Grandpa," I whisper, laying the painting down on the grave. "I brought you a present." Mango immediately walks over and sniffs the edge of the painting. Then he saunters right across it before I can grab him. Now I have to clean the paint off his paws, not to mention paint over the paw prints.

The air is heavy around us and blackish-purple clouds

roll in faster than I had expected. When I was little, I used to run out into the rain and let the water run all over me. Then one day I saw lightning split a tree nearly in half. That pretty much took the joy out of prancing around in thunderstorms. Mango's tail is sinking low, a sure sign that the storm is almost upon us.

I quickly fan out the flowers on Grams's grave and tell Grandpa I miss him and that I hope he likes the painting. I'm about to kneel down to pick it up when the first drops of rain come out of nowhere and splatter right on it. Mango takes off for shelter in the trees, and I freeze while the wind whips up around me. The thunder fills the air with streaks of charcoal-black spirals, and for a split second I think they're trying to pound me into the ground. I turn on my heel and run, leaving the painting with Grandpa.

Wild Child is on the move.

At the edge of the woods I call out for Mango. The woods are awfully dark now, and the rain is really coming down and it's still thundering. What if lightning strikes a tree and it falls on him in the woods? Can he hear me calling him? I don't know what to do. One more clap of thunder makes my mind up for me, and I start running toward home.

When I get back to the house, three things hit me at once. I realize I'm soaked clear through to the bone and am now without both my cat *and* my painting. Why didn't I take my own advice and bring an umbrella? I try to make it upstairs before anyone sees me, but luck is not on my side tonight.

"What happened to *you*?" Beth asks as she follows Dad through the front door and folds up her umbrella. "You look terrible."

"Good to see you too," I say, shivering.

She leans in and gives me a hug. A real one, with affection and everything. She's not wearing any makeup, and her hair is tied back in a ponytail instead of being hair-sprayed out to there. I don't think I've seen her without lipstick on since she was twelve. No makeup, no hair spray, no new piercings, and on top of it a hug? It is all very mysterious and too un-Bethlike. Something's up.

"Want to see what I brought back from California?" she asks, heading upstairs.

She is actually inviting me up to her room. I look at my father for some sign that he recognizes this odd behavior. He's beaming, and I think those might be tears in his eyes. Dad has always been our more sensitive parent. He cries his way through the Olympics and Hallmark commercials. Zack takes after him. He's the only one of us who will offer a dead beetle up to heaven. The rest of us figure bugs have got their own deal worked out.

I follow Beth upstairs and step tentatively into her room, afraid the real Beth will show up any minute and yell at me for trespassing. She rummages through one of her suitcases, pulls out a big plastic bag, and dumps the contents on the bed.

I move closer and my eyes widen. Multicolored candles of all sizes surround bags of tiny flowers and ground herbs, a ceramic goblet, and a tin bowl.

"Are you a good witch or a bad witch?" I ask, fingering the smooth goblet.

"Very funny," she says, snatching the goblet from my hand. "I simply learned to get in touch with the power of nature this summer. Zack's going to help me move my bed around later."

"Move your bed? Why?"

"So my head will face north. It has something to do with the magnetic pull of the North Pole bringing you power while you sleep." She says this as though it makes sense. "I'm sure Zack will help you move yours after."

"But you've always said Zack's superstitions are ridiculous," I remind her as I move away from the bed. Away from the strange objects. Away from the stranger who calls herself my sister.

"I used to say that," she admits, and begins placing the candles around her room. "But now I know there's some truth in them."

"What truth can be found in crossing your fingers until you see a dog?" I mutter, inching toward the door.

"Wait a second," she says. "I'm going to dye my hair tonight, so can you stay out of the bathroom?"

Apparently Beth hasn't changed that much after all. "What color this time?" I ask.

"If you must know," she says, taking out her pony-tail holder so her hair falls perfectly down her back, "it's going to be red. I found out that redheads are closest to nature. You might want to consider—"

"Oh no." I cut her off. "I'm close enough to nature as it is. The bathroom's all yours." I consider inform-ing her that there's hardly any red in nature and that maybe she should try green, but I figure, why start something?

"You're dripping on my carpet," she says. I quickly step out of the room, and she shuts the door behind me.

"Hey!" Beth reappears in the hall two seconds later. This time she's waving her diary in the air. "Did you read this while I was gone?"

The old Beth was definitely back. I suddenly wish I *had* read it. I assure her I did not and run down the hall to my room before she can interrogate me further. I quickly throw off my wet clothes, put on some sweats, and creep down the stairs. The darkest clouds have passed, and only a light drizzle falls now. Just in case, I grab an umbrella and figure the back door is my best chance of escaping unseen. But as I round the corner to the kitchen, I run right into my mother. There are just too many people in this house!

"It's getting dark, Mia," she says, in that special tone that only mothers can achieve. "Where are you going?"

I hesitate. "To the cemetery?"

"You can go tomorrow," she says, taking a bowl of salad out of the refrigerator and handing it to me. "Grandpa isn't going anywhere."

I try to argue but quickly get the mother glare that goes along with the mother tone. The glare and the tone together are unbeatable. I sigh and give up, grimly aware that the painting is probably completely ruined by now. I rest the salad bowl on the counter and turn to leave before I'm asked to set the table. The unmistakable sound of claws against a metal screen door stops me.

I open the kitchen door and Mango strolls in. He is barely wet. Staying dry in the pouring rain is one of those cat tricks I'll never figure out. Instead of apologizing for running off, he heads straight for his food dish and waits for me to fill it.

"Please set the table when you're done, Mia," Mom says, stealing a glance my way. I know she's watching to make sure I don't spill any cat food. Even though I'm a pretty neat person, I'll never be as neat as my mother. She even uses a fork and knife to eat pizza. It's embarrassing. She and Dad are complete opposites that way. I wouldn't exactly call him a slob, but sometimes he trails the outdoors inside with him and Mom has to follow behind him with a mop.

"If the storm passes, I hope to get in a little telescope time," she adds, searching in the back of the cabinet for something. "Do you want to look at Cassiopeia with me? One of the stars in the system is going supernova. When it explodes it will be twenty times brighter than usual."

"Maybe." I have trouble getting excited about a star going supernova. It's an astronomer's way of saying *dying*. Talk about sad on a grand scale. But I know Mom misses being around all her science buddies, and she likes having company in the yard.

"It looks like I have to go to the store to get some spaghetti." Mom slams the cabinet door in exasperation, causing a large brown ring to appear, which reminds me of Beth's old hula hoop. When she was six she won $25 in a contest by hula-hooping longer than any other kid in town. Beth likes winning things.

"Why don't we just have hamburgers?" I suggest as the circle fades away. "We have some in the freezer."

"It's Beth's first night home," Mom tells me, grabbing her keys from the hook by the door. "And she won't eat hamburgers."

"Huh? Since when?" I ask, following her down the hall.

"Since now, apparently," Mom says, her voice strained. "She says she will no longer eat anything with a face. Or anything that once *had* a face."

I'd never thought of meat that way. And I didn't want to start now. I ask my mother to take me with her, figuring I can convince her to stop at the cemetery on the way home. As we drive to the supermarket she reminds me that I still need to get my notebooks and some new clothes for school.

"I still have a week," I point out. I'm not a good shopper. I'd rather be outdoors than cooped up in a mall any day.

"Don't wait till the last minute as usual," she warns. "You've already outgrown a lot of your fall clothes from seventh grade. Once school starts you'll be too busy to get anything."

I'm utterly dreading eighth grade. It means having

to learn a foreign language, not to mention pre-alge-bra, a class I'm destined to fail. No matter how hard I try, I can never keep up in math class, and trying to learn Spanish will be even worse. The problem is clear to me. It has to do with my colors. The word *friend* is turquoise with a glow of glossy red, but the word *amigo* is yellow with spots of brown, like an old banana. I just can't get my brain to connect the two words.

As we stand in line to pay for the spaghetti, I finally agree to go shopping for school stuff the next day. Sat-isfied, my mother turns and strikes up a conversation with the woman behind us. Her son shyly peers out from behind his mother's skirt. He reminds me of Zack at about five years old.

"Hi," I say softly, leaning down to him. "What's your name?"

"Billy Henkle," he answers in a shy whisper. "What's yours?"

"Mia Winchell," I tell him.

He giggles and comes out from behind his mom a little more. "Mia is a pretty name."

"Thanks," I say, flashing him a Winchell smile. My family may not be blessed with height, but we have good teeth and try to show them when we can.

"It's purple with orange stripes," he announces, his voice more assured now. "I like it a lot."

Still smiling, I shake my head and say, "No, silly, it's candy-apple red with a hint of light green." And then what he said hits me. My smile slowly disappears, and my heart starts to pound.

"Wait, what did you say?" I ask him.

Before he can answer, his mother turns around and rolls her eyes. "Don't pay any attention," she tells me. "He has an overactive imagination."

Billy steps back behind her skirt and peeks his head around. "Mia is purple and orange," he whispers. "Not red and green."

I am too stunned to speak. I am too stunned to move. My pulse is beating in my ears. My mother has paid for the food and is already heading toward the exit. I force myself to follow her but can't resist turning around before the door shuts behind me. I hear Billy's mother scolding him for making up stories. The laughter of my classmates pops into my head. *Freeeek.* They made me question the first eight years of my life, and now this little boy is making me question the last five. If he isn't lying, if he really sees my name that way, then everything I thought I knew about myself is wrong.

Chapter Three

I can't sleep. I toss. I turn. Mango tosses and turns with me. Had I misunderstood Billy? Was his mother right? Does he just make things up? After all, my name isn't even remotely purple and orange. The sun streams through the blinds and brings no answers, only more questions. Why does the only person in the world who might see things the way I do have to be five years old? Maybe everyone sees this way at five and I didn't outgrow it. Should I try to find Billy again? What would I say to his mother? All these feelings are rising inside my chest like the foam on the top of a shaken-up soda can. *Bubble, bubble, gurgle.*

I give up on the idea of sleeping and decide to rescue my painting before anyone else wakes up. I completely forgot to ask Mom to stop last night on the way home from the market.

The grass is still covered with dew so I have to be careful not to slip. When I reach the cemetery I stop short and slide about a foot. I'm not alone. I forgot that Jenna and her father come every Wednesday morning.

Right now they're talking to Mrs. Roth, whose family lives on the other side of the valley. The Roths have lived here since the 1800s, and half of the tombstones in the cemetery belong to their ancestors. They're the only Jewish family I know, and every year, they invite the other families in the valley over to light the Hanukkah candles with them. Sometimes they'll call us to say that Mango is in their yard so we won't worry about him. I think he has a crush on one of their female cats. Mrs. Roth steps away to wander among the graves, stopping every few feet to put small rocks on top of her family's headstones.

Jenna joins me at my grandfather's grave. She looks tired. Even her freckles look tired and pale.

"I saw your painting," she says. "Interesting choice to leave it out in the rain."

I look down at it and sigh. The colors have run together quite a bit, and Mango now looks more like a blob with eyes than a kitten. Grandpa's face is still surprisingly intact, although the canvas has creased around him.

"Serves me right," I say, picking up the painting carefully so it won't rip. "I let the rain sneak up on me."

"Do you think you'll be able to fix it?" she asks.

I shake my head. I'm sure I'd be more upset about it if my mind wasn't still focused on meeting Billy last night. I have to force myself not to blurt out the whole story.

"It's a shame," Jenna says. "You worked so hard on it. It looks like it was really good." She squints at it and asks, "Is that a rat on your grandfather's shoulder?"

"Why would I paint a rat on my grandfather's shoulder?"

"How would I know? Maybe he liked rats."

"It's not a rat, Jenna. It's Mango as a kitten!"

"Oh," she says, trying not to smile. "Sorry 'bout that."

Poor Mango has been reduced to a rat. Good thing he isn't around to hear it. "I have to run," I tell Jenna. "My mother's dragging me out for school supplies." As soon as the words are out of my mouth, I regret saying them. Not here, at the cemetery. The last thing I want to do is remind Jenna of one more thing her own mother can't do with her anymore. "Why don't you come with us?" I quickly add.

She shoves her hands into her pockets and shakes her head. "I'm going to spend the day with my dad. Neither of us slept too well last night. Our air conditioning is broken."

I look over at Jenna's father, who is standing by his wife's grave. He is rocking back and forth on his heels, a Chicago Bears cap shielding his eyes.

I don't know what to say now. We both stare at the ground.

"I should get back to him," Jenna says. "I'll call you later."

"Hey, if you want to sleep over tonight you can."

"I'll let you know."

I watch her walk away. These visits are hard for her, no matter what she says. Or doesn't say. I hurry back to the house thinking of all the things we keep from other people. Even our best friends.

⌐

School starts in a few days, and I'm trying to squeeze every last drop out of summer. Literally. I'm squeezing lemons for the lemonade stand Zack and I set up on our street corner.

"Why don't you just use lemonade mix like everyone else?" Beth asks as she passes through the kitchen and into the pantry. She returns with a few sandwich bags and a Magic Marker.

"This is a quality establishment," Zack replies, carefully stirring in the sugar with a long spoon.

"What are the bags for?" I ask as Beth lays them flat on the counter. Zack stops stirring to listen.

"If you must know, I'm sorting herbs for a big project I'm working on."

Zack and I raise our eyebrows at each other.

"If you turn me into a frog, I'm telling Mom and Dad," Zack says, holding the spoon in front of him like a sword.

Beth grunts and turns her back to us. We continue making the lemonade and leave her to her sorcery.

When we are alone again, I ask Zack, "Does the yellow of this lemon remind you of anything?"

"Huh? Like what?"

"Oh, I don't know. Like the letter a or the number four?"

He stops midstir. "What are you talking about?"

"Never mind."

He stares at me as if I'm crazy but cuts the next lemon and starts squeezing. I just had to make sure.

Three hours later we return to the kitchen. We're hot, sunburned, and only four dollars richer. Mom reminds me we have to leave for Mango's vet appointment in fifteen minutes. It takes ten minutes just to find him hiding under my bed. He pretends not to understand me when I explain that the visit is only a routine checkup. I finally spray him with water, and he runs right into the cardboard cat carrier with the picture of a kitten in a spaceship on the side. He no longer gets sick in the car; instead, he complains loudly the whole way into town. Each high-pitched meow sends Sunkist-orange coils dancing in front of me, but I don't mind.

As my mother drives past the supermarket I think of Billy again. Maybe I could go back to the store and ask the clerk if she remembers the Henkle family. Would it do any good? The fact that he might be crazy doesn't make me any *less* crazy.

The noise from the vet's crowded waiting room pours out into the street. As I push open the glass door, a tiny dog with a pushed-in face yips at me in black streaks. Three cats hiss from the relative safety of their cages. I put Mango's carrier on my lap to comfort him. He pokes his nose through one of the round holes on the top, and I pet it while we wait to be called. After signing in, Mom sits down next to me, her nose crinkling up at the smell that always fills the vet's waiting room.

The front door opens, and a boy from school named Roger Carson walks in. He's leading a golden retriever on a tattered leash while his parents follow behind. I don't know him very well, but all during grammar school he wore two different-colored socks. I glance down at his feet. Both of his socks are white today. He doesn't notice me. He won't take his eyes off his dog. The dog looks really old. It can barely hold up its head.

The Carsons gather around their dog, petting it, not looking at any of us. I notice that Roger and his parents and the dog all have various shades of blond hair. I've heard that pets often look like their owners.

I glance at Mango and decide that theory must not be true with cats, since my hair is neither gray nor white. In a flurry of activity, the vet's assistant comes out and ushers Roger's family into the examining room ahead of all the other people who are waiting. Roger's dad asks Roger if he's sure he wants to be here. Roger nods without lifting his head, and the door closes behind them. A minute later I hear whimpering and a bright-blue wail. The whimpering is the dog. The wail is Roger.

"You said it wouldn't hurt him!" he cries, loud enough for us all to hear. "But he's in pain. He's twitching! You said he'd just go to sleep and not feel anything!"

"He's only responding to the needle going in," Roger's father says, his deep voice coming through the wall. The vet adds something in a soothing voice, but I can't make out her words. Roger's sobs, however, are loud and clear and as blue as a swimming pool.

I hug Mango's box tighter, horrified. My breath catches in my throat. All the people in the waiting room draw their pets closer too. My mother reaches over and puts her hand on mine. I close my eyes. *Spirits of dog heaven, I offer the soul of Roger's yellow dog. A good dog, and much loved.* We sit without moving until Roger and his parents come out of the room, their faces wet and red and puffy. No dog. Roger clutches the empty leash to his chest in a tight ball. He notices me this time and his eyes widen. I open my mouth to say something but can't find the words. He gives me a small nod, like he knows I'm trying to say *Oh my God*. My throat feels all closed up.

My mother and I don't talk much on the way home. Mango was very brave when he got his shots. The doctor seemed a little concerned that he was still wheezing. She gave me a new kind of medicine to give him each night to help strengthen his lungs. She warned me it might make him tired.

"That dog was very old," my mother says, breaking the silence between us. "And probably very sick."

"I know," I say, picturing that empty leash as the town fades into country outside the car window. "But still."

"I know," she says.

On Monday, when the school bus pulls up in front of Harrison Middle School, I pray that the first day of school has been canceled because of an earthquake, tidal wave, or avalanche. I'd take any of them. I'm supposed to be one of the big shots this year—the eighth-graders rule the school. But I don't want to rule anybody. And I definitely don't want to take pre-algebra and Spanish. Zack bounds down the steps of the bus, thrilled to be in middle school at last. It's supposed to be the reverse. I'm the one who's supposed to be excited to be in the highest grade, and Zack's the one who is supposed to be cowering in his seat. I glare at his back as I grudgingly follow him off the bus. Jenna and I stand at the bottom of the school steps watching everyone check each other out. Maybe I should have paid more attention to my clothing selection. I glance down at my white shorts and blue T-shirt. It might not be fancy, but at least everything's clean. And I did pull my hair back in a barrette. I'm surprised that Jenna is wearing a dress with tiny pink flowers on it. I can count on one hand the number of times I've seen her in a dress. Her sandals even have small heels on them.

"The same old school, the same old faces," Jenna says with a sigh.

We watch two cheerleaders run up to each other and embrace with a squeal.

Jenna shakes her head. "I really don't think they need to wear their cheerleading outfits on the first day of school. I mean, it's not like they have a game yet."

"School spirit and all that," I tell her as we make our way through the crowd and into the school. "I forgot about your cheerleader phobia."

"I don't have cheerleader phobia," she insists. "I just think the whole concept is sexist and stupid."

At that moment, two boys from our grade run by, hitching up their jeans as they pass us. "Did you see that new cheerleader?" one of them says to the other. "She is h-o-t. Hot!"

Jenna opens her mouth to respond, but the boys are already down the hall. What could she say anyway?

"I hate school," Jenna grumbles as we arrive at her locker.

"No, you don't."

"Well, I at least hate the first day of school. Everyone's trying to impress everyone else."

"Is that why you're wearing a dress?"

"Is it that bad?" she asks, smoothing her skirt.

"No, it's nice," I tell her. "I just haven't seen it before."

"My father bought it for me," Jenna says, tossing her bag lunch into her locker. "You know, as a first-day-of-school thing. I brought shorts and a T-shirt to change into."

"No, you should keep it on," I tell her as the warning bell rings. "And don't go into lunch without me."

"Do I ever?" she calls out, hurrying down the hall to her homeroom.

My first class after homeroom is American history.

History is one of my favorite subjects because I'm good at it. Once I learn the date of a certain event, I can easily remember it by its colors. I remember names the same way.

I'd heard rumors about the serious strangeness of Mrs. Morris, the American history teacher, and I can now say that those rumors are fact. She has a bizarre fear of germs, and as soon as she walks in, she lays down the law.

First she stands by the blackboard and peers at us over her bifocals. Then she says, "Everyone in the front row of desks pick up your books and move to the back. You are to leave the front row empty." The kids in the front row follow her orders, one boy grumbling under his breath that he didn't have cooties the last time he checked.

Mrs. Morris then moves over to her desk and points to two wire baskets. "You are to make two separate piles of homework each day. If you have a cold, you are to place your homework in the pile marked 'ill.' You are to wash your hands before class. With soap. This may sound extreme, but cleanliness is next to godliness." The worst thing about her speech is that her voice is so high-pitched and squeaky that rust-colored spirals rain down behind her.

My next class is English. I like my English teacher,

Mr. Siedler, right away. This is his first year teaching, and he seems pretty nervous. Michelle, the girl who sits behind me and whose father owns the biggest hardware store in town, cracks her gum in my ear. While the teacher is digging through his drawers to find the attendance list, she taps my shoulder and shows me a book on her desk. All I can make out are the words *English Class* written on the brown-bag book cover.

"Did we have a summer reading assignment?" I ask, worried.

She shakes her head and grins slyly. "It's not a schoolbook," she whispers. "It's a *dirty* book. I put the cover on to fool people."

Relieved, I say, "How nice for you," and turn back around in my seat. Note to self: *Don't ask Michelle to be a study partner.* The teacher has us all file up to his desk to pick up the first book on our reading list—*Lord of the Flies.* Why he'd want us to read a book about flies is beyond me.

At lunch a group of boys dare each other to eat the most disgusting combination of cafeteria food. After that, one of them swallows a dime and has to be taken to the school nurse. Jenna and I sit with the same group of girls we've been eating with since fourth grade. Kimberly and Molly, who are best friends but very competitive with each other, and Sara, who is quiet and very serious. As usual, Sara already has her nose buried in a book when we sit down. Kimberly is talking about how she got moved into the honors math class and how next year in high school she's going to be ahead of all the other ninth-graders. I glance at Molly to see if she's going to counter that with anything and am surprised to notice that she was busy over the summer growing breasts. Her tight tank top tells me she has no plans to hide them either. I see Jenna staring too. Molly stands up to find a straw, and I swear at least one boy from each table looks up as she passes. Kimberly sticks out her pointy chin and doesn't look happy. Sara has an amused little smile on her face.

I watch Molly stroll through the maze of tables, but I'm viewing her through a jumble of colors that come together like lumpy oatmeal. The voices and laughter of a hundred kids and various CD players echo off the linoleum walls and fill the air with a collage of colors. It makes it hard to relax and talk to my friends, but the only other option is to sit outside alone and I don't want to do that either.

After lunch I walk with Sara to our pre-algebra class. I have to hurry to keep up with her. "Hey, Sara, wouldn't it be fun if for every two steps we took, we took one backward?"

She doesn't slow her pace even a tiny bit. "Why would we do that?" she asks. "Then we'd be late. Honestly, Mia. You only have one chance to make a first impression."

Who says things like that? I slow down, but she keeps up her breakneck speed. I make it to class right before the bell rings, and the teacher is already writing an equation on the board. I'm sunk already. I just can't grasp how to solve it. Normally an x is a shiny maroon color, like a ripe cherry. But here an x has to stand for an unknown number. But I can't make myself assign the x any other color than maroon, and there are no maroon-colored numbers. Without the color, I don't know how to proceed. I'm lost in shades of gray and want to scream in frustration. I pretend to work on the problem in my notebook. All I write is $x = HELP$ while all over the room hands shoot up to give the answer.

That all-too-familiar combination of confusion and anger is starting to bubble up inside me again. *Gurgle, bubble, sputter.*

Spanish class isn't any better. I try to match the colors of the English words to the new Spanish words. *Hello* and *hola* works fine. *Mother* and *madre* is a bit of a stretch, but it is close enough that I can remember it. *Boy* and *chico* doesn't work at all. Neither does *girl* and *chica*, *good* and *bueno*. *Adiós* and *good-bye* to the honor roll. At least I know that one.

The only good part of the day is my last class. As soon as I walk into the art room and pick a stool at one of the worktables, I feel like I'm home. All of the art students had to be approved by the teacher before they could get into the class, just like last year and the year before. The same kids always make it. While I'm looking around the room, a young woman walks in carrying a huge pile of books in her arms. She tells us to call her Karen. Just Karen. A smooth plum-colored name with little yellow specks. It takes me a minute to figure out she's the teacher. The girl next to me raises her hand, and Karen looks up from passing out the books.

"Um, what happened to Mrs. Simpson?" she asks tentatively.

I am wondering the same thing. Mrs. Simpson had been the art teacher for something like thirty years.

Karen looks around and then says with a sigh, "Mrs. Simpson went on to a better place."

"She *died?*" the girl exclaims in horror.

The class emits a collective gasp. I grab onto the edge of the table.

Karen shakes her head. "No, no. She went to the high school. She teaches there now. My teaching methods are a little different from hers, but I have a feeling you'll enjoy yourselves."

Now everyone lets out a sigh of relief. I think Mrs.

Simpson will be happier at the high school. She was always muttering about middle-school hormones running amok. Although I would think high-school hormones were even worse.

Karen tells us to look through the new art book and pick an artist whose style we want to imitate. She says we'll learn a lot about our own style by studying others. I'd like to think I have a style already, but I guess it couldn't hurt to study someone else's. I flip through the pages, but nothing jumps out at me.

When school is over I meet Jenna at her locker, the same as I've done every day after school since we were old enough to have lockers. She's still in the dress, but she's wearing her sneakers from gym instead of the sandals.

"This has got to go," she says. In one motion she rips out the poster that had been inside her locker door for two years. "Boy bands are so over. What was I thinking?"

We pass my history classroom, and Jenna ducks in and throws the crumpled poster in the garbage can. A plan forms in my head. I lean close and whisper in her ear. "PIC mission."

She nods and awaits instructions.

"You wait here at the door," I tell her. "Drop your book bag if someone's coming."

"Okay, but hurry. I don't want to miss the bus on the first day of school."

I look both ways, dash into the room, and head straight for the teacher's desk. In one swift maneuver, I switch the sick and healthy baskets.

"Mission accomplished," I announce upon my return. We turn and run outside to where the buses pick us up. We figure out which is ours, and Jenna gets on first. When I reach the top stair I hear a small voice yell out, "Hi, Mia!" I turn around in time to see Billy Henkle waving excitedly from the window of a passing car. He must have an older brother or sister in middle school! By the time I collect my senses to wave back, the bus driver has shut the door behind me. Jenna picks a seat in the back, and I slide in after her. I have a hard time paying attention to what she's saying. It would be easier to pretend I never met Billy and to forget about my colors. As the bus rolls out into the country, I decide to try. I'm going to be so normal that when people look up *normal* in the dictionary, my name will be there.

Chapter Four

Only two weeks into school and I've already failed two math quizzes. Failed with a bright-purple capital *F*. The note from my teacher is burning a hole in my back pocket, and I know I should give it to my parents. Instead, I'm sitting at the kitchen table forcing myself to finish the rest of my homework. Zack is actually humming as he does his sixth-grade long division. Beth claimed she didn't have any homework and is outside gathering herbs in the moonlight. I can't remember ever seeing Beth in the woods before. She isn't the outdoorsy type, which is pretty pathetic considering our house is surrounded by fields and woods. Mango is on my lap, purring away as I pet him.

I finish reading the third chapter of *Lord of the Flies*, which, it turns out, is not about flies at all. I can't help yawning. Reading always makes me tired because sometimes I get so caught up in the rainbowlike colors of the words that I have to read passages over and over.

"You really should cover your mouth when you yawn," Zack says.

"Why? We're not in public."

He shrugs and resumes his homework. "It's your soul, not mine."

"My soul?" I ask. "Since when do you know about souls?"

"Oh, I know about souls," he says gravely. "And I know that if you yawn and don't cover your mouth, your soul can jump out."

I stare at him. "Where did you hear that? The Internet again?"

"It's common knowledge," he says.

"You're as strange as they come, Zack."

"Thanks."

"It isn't a compliment," I assure him.

"It is to me," he says.

I return to the sheet of math equations in front of me. After staring at the swirls of gray for five full minutes, I finally throw my pencil across the room in disgust. Mango jumps off my lap and chases halfheartedly after the pencil before lying down to wash himself. I am not a stupid person. I know I'm not. Why can't I figure out this basic math problem? Zack peers at me in surprise.

"Something wrong?" he asks. At least that's what I think he says. The frustration blots out everything so that all I can focus on is this weird heaviness in my chest. The bubbling up inside me has gotten too strong. I can feel it rising to the surface. *Bubble, bubble, simmer, fizz,* and *BOOM!* So much for trying to be normal. That didn't last long.

I push back my chair, ignore the rusty-red scraping sound that reminds me of dried blood, and march into the living room. My parents are sitting together on the couch trying to decide if they should be worried about Beth's new hobby. They stop talking when they see me.

Okay. Deep breath. Here goes. Just blurt it out. I wish Grandpa were here. He would know exactly what to do.

"I have to tell you guys something." Once the words are out, I am unable to make my lips work again.

They wait for me to continue, and I almost chicken out. But the *BOOM* is still ringing in my ears. I have no choice but to remind them of the one incident in my life I'd hoped everyone had forgotten. I take another deep breath. "Remember in third grade when you guys had to come to the principal's office to get me?"

They think for a few seconds. Then my father says, "Something about chalk?"

"Right," I say. "Chalk." And at that moment I taste the chalk in my mouth, feel it tickling my throat.

"What about it?" my mother asks.

"Well, remember I told everyone I made the whole thing up?"

"Vaguely," she says. "What's this all about, Mia?"

"Well, the thing is," I begin, knowing there is no turning back now, "I wasn't lying. Numbers really *do* have colors for me. So do letters and sounds."

They are staring at me with that familiar Mia-sprouted-another-head stare, but I keep talking. I bounce around the room as I speak. Each word lightens me a bit more.

"I used to think everyone saw these colors; then in third grade I figured out it was just me." My mind flashes to Billy for a second, but I don't want to confuse things even more. Not until I figure out what his story is. "I thought I should tell you about it before I get two F's on my report card." I dig into my pocket and hand my mom the crumpled note. "You have to sign this."

I plop down on the armchair across from them, waiting for their reaction as they read the note together. I don't have to wait too long.

"Is this whole story some kind of joke to justify your difficulty with math?" asks my mother with a frown. "Because it wasn't funny in third grade and it isn't funny now."

"It isn't a joke, Mom," I reply, gritting my teeth.

My father studies me for a minute. "Do you mean to say you hallucinate?"

I shake my head. "It's not like that."

"*Hallucinating* means you imagine you see things that aren't there," my father adds.

I try not to lose my patience. "I know what the word means, Dad. But I'm not imagining things. My colors are as real as this house."

"What kinds of colors are these, exactly?" my mother asks. I can tell she's still not sure whether I'm lying.

I try to think of the easiest way to describe it. "Each letter and number has its own color," I explain. "Like a k is turquoise blue, whether I think of it, read it, or hear it. It's just there, inside my head, plain as day."

They continue to stare at me, and I begin to squirm.

"Sounds have colors too," I add, figuring there's no use holding anything back at this point. "High-pitched sounds give the sharpest colors. When I hear a noise, I'll see the color and shape that go with—"

"Shape?" my father interrupts.

"Yes, shape," I say. "The colors appear in geometric shapes like spirals or balls or zigzags, that sort of thing. Or sometimes just a hazy patch of colored air."

"Does this block your vision?" my mother asks hurriedly. "Does it hurt?"

I shake my head at both questions. "No, it's not like that really. It's more—"

"This is all your fault," my mother informs my father before I can finish my sentence.

"My fault?" He jumps up from the couch. "How are you blaming this on me?"

"All those drugs in the sixties," she says accusingly.

"What drugs?" he sputters. "I never took drugs in the sixties."

"Well, neither did I," she says.

"I never said you did."

This conversation has taken an unexpected turn, and my head is going back and forth like a Ping-Pong ball.

"Your brother used drugs," she says matter-of-factly, unwilling to give up this line of reasoning.

"What does that have to do with me? Or Mia?" he demands.

"Maybe you inhaled something and passed it on to her," she says. "Or, or—"

"*Or*, maybe this is your crazy aunt Polly's fault," my father responds. "Maybe Mia inherited something from her."

"My aunt Polly isn't crazy," my mother says defensively. "She's just a little eccentric. That has nothing to do with—"

"I figured you'd think I'm crazy," I say, trying to keep my voice steady. They glare at each other, and then both their faces soften.

"We don't think you're crazy, Mia," my father says, sitting down again. "We just don't understand." He reaches over and takes my hands in his. "Do you remember when this started?"

"It's always been there," I tell him, still stinging from their words.

"I bet I know what this is all about," my mother says excitedly. "I bet it's those building blocks you used to play with. You know, the ones with the colored letters on them?"

"Huh?" I say.

"You probably memorized the colored letters when you were a baby," she says. "And you've been associating colors with letters and numbers ever since."

I think about that for a second, then shake my head. "That can't be it," I say. "That doesn't explain—"

"I'll run down to the basement and get them," she says, ignoring me. "I'm sure they're still in the old toy chest."

She's off and running before I can stop her. My father and I just look at each other. Time passes very slowly until she returns.

Cradling a few dusty blocks in her arms, she holds one up in front of me. It has the letter q carved on each side in faded red. "What color is this?" she asks.

"It's red," I tell her.

"See!" she says gleefully. "I'm right!"

"The *q* is red," I repeat, "on the *block*. But in my head it's a dark silver, like the color of Dad's helicopter."

My mother doesn't say anything. She just keeps turning the block over and over in her hand.

"Well," my father says after a long pause, "we'll just have to go see Dr. Randolph. I'm sure he'll be able to help."

Over the years, Dr. Randolph has cured us kids of everything from chicken pox to broken bones. He means well, but he's getting old and a little forgetful. For the last few years, he's called me Beth. I even heard him call *Zack* Beth once, but Zack denies it.

"Dad, the last time we went to Dr. Randolph you said he wasn't the sharpest tool in the shed anymore."

"Never mind that," he says. "We have to start somewhere. I'll call him right now."

He goes into the kitchen and opens the cabinet with

the emergency numbers posted on it. Mom is still staring at the block, as if she's trying to see what I see. I know how frustrating it is to see something differently from someone else, or in my case, *everyone* else, and I feel sorry for her.

I have to go give Mango his pill, so I stand up to leave. Mom breaks her gaze away from the block and looks at me solemnly.

"Why didn't you come to us before?" she asks. She sounds hurt.

My throat tightens. "I tried to, back in third grade. No one believed me, remember?"

"I'm glad you're telling us now," she says, reaching out to hug me. It feels good. Mom's not usually the touchy-feely type.

"We'll find out what's going on," she assures me. "Don't worry."

I nod and leave her holding the q up to the light.

Mango is asleep on my bed, wheezing his mango wheeze contentedly. He springs up as soon as I open the box of tuna-flavored cat treats. Without my colors, Mango's wheezes would just be wheezes with no comforting mango puffs. Is that worth giving up for good grades? I guess I have no choice. After all, everyone else manages just fine without seeing them. He gobbles down the treat, never suspecting a pill is hidden inside it. He's so trusting. I give him a few more treats without pills in them, and then he yawns in my face and I wave away his icky tuna breath.

That night, I go to bed early and dream that Dr. Randolph has turned Mango into a stack of dusty building blocks. Every time I pile them up, someone comes and knocks them back down.

I can never turn around fast enough to see who it is.

By morning my parents are still waiting to hear from Dr. Randolph, so they decide to send me off to school. On the bus I randomly open my art book to an artist I haven't seen before. I decide instantly that this is the guy for me. His name is Kandinsky, and the shapes he uses in his paintings look a lot like the ones I see when I hear noises. His images are all twisted together and overlapping, like when I hear music with a lot of different instruments. The colors he uses are flatter, more primary than the ones I usually see, but they're still pretty close.

In history we are divided into groups of four and told that each group will have to present a big project at the end of the marking period. It will be based on an event in American history that America would rather forget. Roger Carson is in my group, along with Jonah Finley and Laura Hoffson, who is always the first to volunteer the answer in class. Roger and I glance at each other, and he quickly looks down at his desk. We're supposed to get together outside of school to decide the topic. Half of our grade will depend on this assignment, but no one seems too eager to make plans. Least of all me. The marking period isn't over until Thanksgiving, and that seems very far away right now.

During lunch Jenna tells us about the boy-girl party she's planning for her birthday in November. Molly starts pointing at the boys she thinks should be invited, when the school guidance counselor shows up at our table.

"You're Mia Winchell, right?" she asks me.

Surprised, I nod. Had I done something wrong? Had I put my history homework in the wrong pile?

"Your mother is here," she informs me. Then she lowers her voice and says, "You have an appointment with your doctor."

I gather my books while the guidance counselor waits.

"It's nothing," I assure my friends. "I'll see you later."

My mother is waiting on the front steps of the school, and she tells me Dr. Randolph has agreed to see me right away. For some reason Beth is in the front seat of the car, her newly red hair glowing unnaturally in the sunlight.

"What's *she* doing here?" I ask.

"She has poison ivy all over her arms and legs," my mother informs me, holding open the back door. "Be nice."

I slide in and lean forward, noting that Beth has tube socks on both her arms. "So, how'd the herb-picking go, Beth?"

"Shut up."

"Can't you just cast a spell and make the poison ivy go away?" I ask.

"Mom!" Beth says.

"Mia," my mother warns.

I lean back in my seat. "Sorry."

Beth looks at me over her shoulder. "Why are you going to Dr. Randolph anyway? You don't look sick."

I don't know what to say. Luckily Mom jumps in and says I just need a checkup. Beth doesn't seem convinced, but she drops it and starts scratching the back of her hand through the socks. Mom tells her to stop or she'll get scars. That stops her instantly.

Dr. Randolph's waiting room reminds me of the vet's except with kids instead of animals. A group of toddlers play with toy trains and Legos while a baby hollers in his mother's arms. I cover my ears to soften the shrill screams, but it doesn't stop the silver spears from shooting across the room. I wish everyone else could see them. At least here I'm not the only one covering my ears. I'm dreading going in there and having to explain everything again.

The three of us sit as far away from the chaos as possible. Beth has started scratching again. I make sure I don't get too close.

"Why do you still bring us to a baby doctor?" Beth asks our mother. I am wondering the same thing.

Mom frowns. "Dr. Randolph is a pediatrician," she says. "That means he sees children of all ages. Including sixteen-year-olds and thirteen-year-olds."

Beth is finally called in, and my mother starts to get up with her.

"That's okay," Beth tells her. "I can do this on my own." My mother sits back down with a sigh.

"By the way, Mia, I spoke to your math teacher this morning."

I try to ignore the toddler pawing at my sneaker. "You did? What did she say?"

"She doesn't understand why you're having so much trouble, since you do so well in most of your other classes. She said if you don't improve you'll have to go to summer school next year."

"You're kidding me."

"I wish I were."

"What am I going to do?" I ask. Nothing could be worse than summer school.

"We'll figure something out," she promises. "I'll go over your homework with you."

I don't have the heart to tell her it's not going to help. I know what I'm supposed to do to solve the equations; somehow I just manage to get all mixed-up in the middle.

Ten minutes later Beth returns covered in pink lotion, clutching a prescription. She doesn't look happy. The nurse pokes her head out of the door and motions me in. I wait for my mother to join me. There's no way I'm going in there alone.

Dr. Randolph meets us in the examination room. I hop up on the table and wait for him to cure me. He's always done it before. He finishes flipping through my file and then turns to me.

"Hi, Mia," he says, smiling his friendly-neighbor-hood-doctor smile. "How are we today?"

I look at my mother, and she gestures for me to answer.

"I'm fine," I tell him, relieved he remembered my name.

"Your father told me what's been going on with

you," he says. "And I have to admit, it has me puzzled."

My shoulders drop, and my mother's face falls a little.

"But I'll do my darndest to figure it out," he says, and I allow myself a small surge of hope.

He proceeds to give me a regular exam, checking my ears, eyes, throat, and reflexes. He listens to my lungs and heart with a cold stethoscope and even tickles my feet to see if I feel it. I do.

Then he asks if I've started menstruating yet.

I feel my face start to burn. I don't see what that has to do with anything. "No," I reply, looking away. I think many girls in my class have their periods already, but as far as I'm concerned there is no rush to cross that threshold into womanhood. It sure hasn't made Beth any nicer. After that day in fifth grade when the boys were sent out of the room to play kickball and the girls had to learn about becoming a woman, Jenna and I swore we'd never get our periods. So far, so good.

Dr. Randolph makes some notes in his file and scratches his head. Then he weighs me, measures my height, and has me bend over so he can see if my spine is straight. I keep glancing at my mother, but she is wearing her just-be-patient face.

Suddenly he opens the door and slams it. My mother and I both jump.

Dr. Randolph turns to me. "So," he says. "What did you see?"

It takes me a few seconds to realize this is a test. "I saw brown rings," I tell him.

"Where?" he asks.

"About three feet away from me, in the air."

"Just hanging there in space?" he asks.

Did I sense an edge of disbelief creeping into his voice? "Just hanging there," I say.

"Are they still there?" he asks. His eyes flicker toward my mother.

"No," I tell him. "The colors and shapes only last about two seconds unless the noise keeps going."

"What color is the word *doctor?*" he asks.

I answer without hesitation. "It's mostly hot pinkish purple because that's the color of the d, but the colors of the other letters add a gold tinge to it. Oh, and it's also kind of grainy."

"Anything else?" he asks wearily.

I think for a minute. "Nope, that's all." I cross my arms and wait for the next question. Instead he motions for my mother to step into the hall with him. I wonder if I failed the test somehow.

A minute later they're back. "Well, Beth," Dr. Randolph begins, "I think it will be best if—"

"Mia." I correct him, ignoring my mother's glare.

"What?" he asks.

"My name," I say clearly, "is Mia."

"Of course it is," he says defensively. "Now, as I was just telling your mother, I think it will be best if you see a psychotherapist. I've given your mother the name of a young woman who I'm sure will be able to help you." With that he ushers us out the door and back down the hall.

My head hangs low. I feel deflated, as though the air is slowly leaking out of me. "So he thinks I'm crazy too," I say to my mother as we rejoin the fray in the waiting room.

"No, he doesn't," she says softly so Beth won't hear. "He's just trying to help." Beth hops up when she sees us. The lotion flakes off her as we walk to the car. If I didn't feel so sorry for myself, I would feel pretty bad for her.

"If Dr. Randolph doesn't think I'm crazy, then why is he sending me to a therapist?" I ask my mother as we walk to the entrance of my school together. "I watch television. I know what therapists do."

"Dr. Randolph only wants you to get better. He believes this is the next step."

"He called me Beth again," I remind her.

"It could have been worse," she says, turning to go. "He could have called you Zack."

At that point I would rather have been called anything but crazy. It is one thing for me to call myself crazy. It is another thing entirely when a doctor does it.

I pull open the heavy front door right as the bell rings at the end of sixth period. I blend in with the throng and make my way to gym class. Running around the track always makes me feel better. I quickly change into my gym clothes and am the first one out on the field. I may be crazy, but at least I can run fast. The other kids eventually file out, and the track fills up. As I pass Roger on the track I decide he must have outgrown his two-different-socks phase. Just as I make this observation, he trips and lands hard on his side. Two kids help him off the field, and he hobbles back inside. After I change into my regular clothes, I find him sitting on the bleachers with an ice pack on his left ankle.

"Are you okay?" I ask.

He looks up and grimaces a little. "I twisted my ankle pretty bad. I could have sprained it."

"If you wanted to get out of gym class, there are easier ways."

He smiles, and I think he must have gotten his braces off recently because his teeth look very straight.

"We need to get together about the history project," he says, steadying the ice pack, which had begun to slip. "I'll give you my number, and we can make plans over the phone." With his free hand he reaches in his book bag and hunts around for a pencil. I notice he has a paperback copy of one of the Narnia books.

"Have you read that yet?" I ask him as he pulls out the book and leans on it to write his phone number.

"At least ten times," he says, handing me the scrap of paper with his number on it. "They're my favorite books. Have you read them?"

"I've only read the first one," I tell him. "I'm not too big on reading."

A brief look of disappointment flickers across his face. For some reason I feel like I need to explain. "Reading is hard for me sometimes, that's all. It's not that I don't like it."

"Oh," Roger says, clearly unsure of what else to say. The bell rings and startles both of us.

"Call me tonight about the project, okay?"

I nod as I hurry out of the gym. I don't picture myself calling him any time soon.

Jenna tries very hard not to pry on the bus after school. She talks about the weather, how it should be cooling off a bit. She tells me her gym teacher made the girls cheer for the boys in volleyball and that she's going to file a complaint.

When the driver lets us out at our stop, she can't hold it in anymore. "I know you'd tell me if something was wrong," she says, "because best friends tell each other everything, right?"

"Can we talk about it later?" I ask. "It's kind of a long story, and I need to start my art project."

"Just tell me one thing. Are you sick?"

"No, I'm not sick." *Am I?* "I promise I'll tell you everything later."

"Later like when?" she asks.

"This weekend," I hear myself saying.

"Okay," she says reluctantly. "But I'm going to hold you to it."

"I know," I say, wondering if there is any chance she'll forget. Not likely.

When I get home I close myself in my room and set up my easel. As if on cue, my father starts hammering. If I'm going to imitate Kandinsky, I'm going to have to bring on the shapes. I turn on the radio to a heavy rock station and also put in a cassette of a thunderstorm. The shapes come unbidden, as always, and I begin to paint. It's a good thing this assignment was given early in the year. After all, my colors and shapes may not be around much longer if I can actually find a doctor to cure me. I should record them for posterity—a word I only recently learned means the people who come after you in history, not your rear end, which is your *posterior.*

I concentrate hard and paint fast to keep up with the fleeting images. As soon as I try to capture one in my head, it's gone and morphed into another shape. After an hour I stand back and admire my progress. It actually looks a lot like Kandinsky's work. But I bet he didn't get a headache from all the noise! I paint and paint until I fill up almost every available space on the canvas. When I turn off the music, the resulting quiet is a big relief. I lie down on the bed and let the silence seep into me like a cool breeze.

Saturday afternoon rolls around all too quickly, and Jenna waits impatiently for me to start talking. The gray sky looks slightly threatening. I keep glancing up as we find our favorite log at the edge of the woods. I run my finger over the words *Mia and Jenna's Log, Keep Away*, which we carved into the soft bark a few summers ago using my father's pocketknife. One of our first PIC missions was snagging the knife from his toolshed and then returning it, undiscovered.

Jenna swings her legs back and forth, side to side, wordlessly willing me to speak. I had hoped to be able to tell her I'd been cured so I wouldn't have to go into the details, but I still haven't seen the therapist. Apparently a lot of other people in town have mental problems, because I can't get an appointment until Monday.

I watch ants file neatly into the ant hole by my feet and remind myself that Jenna and I have known each other forever. She is closer to me than my own sister. Much closer actually. I open my mouth and force myself to start talking. Breathlessly, I tell her about seeing colors and about how I thought everybody saw things that way and then I found out that nobody did and I felt so alone and strange. I tell her I wasn't lying that day I got sent home in third grade. She's not saying anything, so I ramble on, my hands flying around in the air. "I've always wanted to tell you that your first name is the color and texture of wet grass. And your last name is purplish pink and white, like a peppermint candy. Grass and peppermint, isn't that nice?" As I say that I realize how cool Jenna is, and I wonder how

I could have been afraid to tell her all these years. I wait for her response. When it comes it almost knocks me off the log.

She bursts out crying.

"Jenna?" I say, my eyes opening wide. "What's wrong?"

She turns her face away and wipes her eyes with the back of her hand. I can see the tears are sliding down her cheeks. She sniffles and wipes again. I feel totally helpless. Finally she faces me again.

"I can't believe you hid this from me for all these years," she says with an unfamiliar hardness in her voice. "I've shared everything with you. Everything! Why didn't you tell me?"

Shocked by her reaction, my words flow out strangely. "But nobody knows...I kept it from everybody. I got used to keeping it to myself. Please don't take it personally." I'm practically begging her now.

She stands up. "How can I not? I thought you were my best friend."

"I am," I say, jumping up from the log. "And you're mine. We're Partners in Crime!" My eyes fill with tears. This hasn't gone at all as I expected. My head is reeling.

"Maybe you don't know what a best friend is." She steps away from me.

My jaw falls open. "Maybe *you* don't. I thought if anyone would understand it would be you."

"Well, I don't understand," she says angrily. "I don't understand why you didn't tell me in third grade. Or fourth grade. Or seventh. It's always been you and me against the world. I'll bet there are lots of things you don't bother to tell me."

"There aren't," I insist. Jenna and I had never fought before. Ever. I can feel my hands start to shake.

"I have to go home," Jenna says suddenly. She hurries along the path back to our houses. I run to the edge of the woods and wait for her to look back, but she doesn't. I'm so shocked, I don't know what to feel. As I walk home I decide on anger. By the next morning, I change my mind and choose disappointment. And after school on Monday, after Jenna had ignored me all day, I decide on very, very hurt.

Chapter Five

The fight with Jenna is still playing over in my head as my mother leads me into the therapist's office. This waiting room is completely different from Dr. Randolph's. No crying babies, no scratching sisters. The doctor's schedule is supposedly full, but the room is completely empty, silent as a tomb. The oversized chairs are white; the walls, covered with occasional landscape paintings, are white; and the plush carpet is the whitest of all. I'm insanely glad I didn't bring a cup of grape juice with me.

On the wall above the magazine rack is a row of light switches with different names under them. My mother scans them until she finds the one marked "Finn." She then flicks the switch to the On position.

"What's that for?" I ask in a whisper. I'm afraid to make any noise in this quiet, white place.

"Dr. Finn told me to do that when we arrived," she says. "A light turns on in her office so she knows to come get us."

I sit in one of the chairs and sink down deep. My

feet don't even reach the floor. This office doesn't feel like a place for crazy people. At least not a place for crazy people with grape juice. I have the uneasy feeling we're being watched. If there had been a moose head on the wall, I swear the eyes would have been moving. My hands get that numb feeling.

"Mom," I whisper from the depths of my chair, "do you think they have a hidden video camera focused on us? You know, to see what we're like before we go in there?"

"No, I don't," she replies. "I wish you'd just relax. Dr. Finn only wants to talk to you."

"At least *someone* wants to talk to me," I mutter.

"What do you mean?" my mother asks, shifting around in her own plush chair. "Who's not talking to you?"

I sigh and say, "Jenna. She hasn't spoken to me since Saturday. I told her about what's going on, and I don't know, she just freaked out because I hadn't told her before. She didn't say a word to me in school today."

"You know how sensitive Jenna is," my mother says. "But she'll come around, you'll see."

I don't know what I'd do if she didn't. There isn't anyone else I would want for a best friend. I twist the friendship bracelet back and forth on my wrist. Molly and Kimberly and Sara are fine for school friends, but we've never spent much time together outside of school. We all live too far from each other. I wish Mango were here with me, his dirty paws leaving little tracks on the white carpet. I haven't seen much of him this week. I think he's been hanging out at the Roths' house lately, sniffing around their new cat, Twinkles. I don't know which is more embarrassing: Mango having a crush on the cat, or the fact that the cat's name is Twinkles.

A few minutes later the door opens, and a tall woman who looks like she's in her late thirties enters. She walks over to me and holds out her hand.

"You must be Mia," she says. Her voice is sweet and makes me think of whipped cream, which reminds me that I was too upset to eat lunch today and could use some food.

I nod.

"I'm Ms. Finn," she says, bending over to shake my hand. "Let's go into my office and get to know each other."

"Isn't it Dr. Finn?" my mother asks.

Ms. Finn smiles and says, "I'm a psychotherapist, not a psychologist. Many people make that mistake. I assure you the level of care is the same."

I'm still stuck in the deep chair and have to use both hands to push myself out. My mother starts to follow us out the door, but Ms. Finn stops her.

"This is usually best without the mothers," she says. My mother has no choice but to stay behind. I pause at the doorway and look back pleadingly, but my mother waves me on.

Feeling alone and unsure, I follow Ms. Finn into a small office that is very similar to the waiting room. Only this room has framed diplomas on the walls and a bowl of jelly beans on a big mahogany desk. A box of tissues is conveniently placed next to the plush couch where Ms. Finn instructs me to "sit, relax, make yourself at home." The tissues are a bad sign. Either she expects me to cry or to sneeze a lot. At least I don't sink in quite as deep this time when I sit down. My toes just reach the rug. I can only gaze longingly at the jelly beans, which are about a foot too far away to reach. My stomach growls.

"Now, Mia," Ms. Finn begins in a firm voice. All traces of the whipped cream have disappeared. "Dr. Randolph has filled me in on your situation. Maybe together, you and I can figure out what is causing you to see these colors."

I nod cautiously.

She continues. "I'm a very straightforward person.

Another therapist might be the 'silent type,' but I call it like I see it, all right?"

"Okay."

"Do you see the colors when you're mad at your parents?"

"I don't usually get mad at my parents," I tell her honestly, my eyes drifting back to the bowl of jelly beans. "That's my older sister's job."

"Remember, Mia, anything you say in here is confidential."

I nod. Unfortunately, my only secret is already out.

"I need to ask if you've ever taken drugs," Ms. Finn says, looking me straight in the eye, daring me to lie. "Anything that might have caused these colors as a side effect."

Taken aback, I tell her no, I've never taken drugs. I don't even like to take medicine when I'm sick.

She jots something down on her notepad.

"Now, Mia, what is your place in the birth order of your family?"

"I have one older sister and a younger brother. But they don't see things like I do."

She taps her pen rapidly on her desk and asks, "Are you familiar with middle child syndrome?"

I shake my head. I don't like the sound of anything that ends with the word *syndrome*.

"Let me see if I can explain," she says, her voice suddenly soothing again. "Middle children are in an unfortunate position. They get neither the privileges reserved for the first born nor the special attention specific to the baby of the family. Do you follow me?"

"I understand what you're saying," I tell her, trying not to sound defensive. "But I don't think it's like that in my family. My parents don't treat us any differently."

"Who has the largest bedroom?" Ms. Finn asks bluntly.

"Beth does," I admit. "But that's only because she was here first, you know; she was already in there when I was born."

"And who does your mother spend the most time with?"

"Zack, I guess," I say, feeling slightly defeated. "But that's because she has to do things with him that Beth and I can do on our own. He's only eleven."

"So you see what I'm saying?" she asks, leaning back in her chair. "Middle children can feel neglected, often for good reasons. Or they feel that they aren't as special as the other children, or even as loved. When that happens, middle children often act out."

"Act out?" I repeat suspiciously.

"A child may devise an elaborate plan to get his or

her parents' attention," she explains. "Something that will make her stand out from the other siblings."

I do not like where this is heading.

"Something," she continues, "like telling her parents that she sees colors all the time. Colors that no one else, including her brother and sister, can see." She leans forward and waits for my response.

My heart sinks—a feeling I'm becoming all too familiar with. Another doctor who doesn't believe me. Whatever happened to innocent until proven guilty?

"That's not it," I assure her, aware that I'm losing the battle to stay calm. "I am not making this up to get attention. I don't even *like* getting attention. I just want to figure out what's wrong with me."

She nods thoughtfully and scribbles some more notes. "Tell me, Mia," she says, "do you often get depressed for no reason?"

"No."

"Do you get enough sleep?"

"Yes."

"Any trouble making friends?"

"No." Keeping them is another story, but I don't tell her that.

"And these colors and shapes, they feel real to you?"

"Very real."

She looks at me steadily. "Well, then," she says, "why don't I talk to your mother for a while? We'll see what she has to say."

As she leads me out of her office, I swipe three jelly beans from the bowl.

When we reach the still-empty waiting room, I trade places with my mother. I wait until I hear Ms. Finn's door close behind her, then tiptoe down the hall and stand outside her office.

I put my ear as close to the door as I can without touching it. The first thing I hear is my mother exclaim, "A brain tumor?"

I jump back against the wall; my eyes open wide. Does Ms. Finn think I have a brain tumor? Isn't that what people in soap operas get before they die young and still beautiful? The grape-flavored jelly bean in my mouth suddenly tastes flat.

"I'm sure that's not it, Mrs. Winchell," she assures my mother and, without her realizing it, me. "A neurologist does a lot more than test for brain tumors. If Mia's problem is real and not in her imagination, then a neurologist will be able to test her brain functions."

Relieved but still shaken, I return to the relative safety of my deep chair. It sucks me in again, but this time I don't mind. So another doctor will poke and prod and then send me to someone else. Why did I get myself into this?

I pick up the magazine my mother left on the table and open to a page full of text. As I read, a rainbow of colors drifts by in my head. I close my eyes and watch the colors fade away. I imagine that when I open my eyes again all the letters are black, the color of the type they are printed in, and nothing more.

I open my eyes and stare at the page. I see the black letters. But I also see the pinks and greens and purples and yellows. I can't say I'm surprised.

My mother ducks her head in the waiting room. "Let's go, Mia." By the time I push myself out of the chair, she's halfway down the hall. I hurry to catch up.

"So what's going on?"

Without turning to look at me, she says, "Ms. Finn gave me the number of a neurologist at the University of Chicago. He's going to run some tests."

"What kinds of tests?" I ask as we head out to the car. "Is something wrong with my brain?"

She finally stops walking and turns to me. "Nothing is wrong with your brain, Mia."

I size her up as she stands by the car, searching her purse for the keys. "But you don't know for sure, do you?"

She keeps digging in her bag. "I suppose I don't."

"Mom?"

"What?" she answers, not quite snapping at me, but almost.

"You already put the key in the car door." I point to the keys dangling from the lock.

After that we don't talk much. I keep peeking over at her on the ride home, but she has a sort of pinched expression on her face. This worries me more than anything else. My head feels very heavy. I flip down the visor and stare at the small mirror. I never thought of my brain as anything other than the place where thoughts came from. Now it's this big heavy thing rattling around in there—all mushy and gray and, I don't know, *brainlike*. I move my fingers around my skull.

"What are you doing?" Mom asks with a sideways glance.

"I read somewhere that doctors used to feel the bumps on people's heads to tell what was wrong with them." I keep searching but don't feel anything unusual.

"Don't worry, Mia. Everything will be fine."

"I won't worry if *you* won't worry."

"I'm not worried," she says.

"Me either then."

"Good."

"Good," I echo.

"So neither of us is worried," she says.

"Right."

Then we look at each other and the corners of our mouths twitch. I start laughing and she joins me. It's better than crying.

⌁

"You don't have a brain tumor!" my mother says, shaking me awake. Dad stands behind her, beaming.

"What?" I rub my eyes and look at my wall clocks. 6:10 A.M. Mango yawns and stretches at the foot of the bed.

"How do you know? I haven't even had the tests yet." Suddenly panic grips me. I sit up and grab my mother by the sleeve of her nightshirt. "Or did I have them and the doctor took out the memory part of my brain?"

They laugh. "No, you didn't have them," my mother assures me. "I just got off the phone with the neurologist."

"At six o'clock in the morning?"

She sits down on the edge of the bed. "He's at a conference in Europe, where it's already the afternoon. He got the message I left yesterday and wanted to reassure us. He said that since you've had this condition your whole life without any other neurological impairments, he can rule out diseases such as epilepsy or tumors."

I lean back on the pillow as relief washes over me. "What else did he say?"

"He said he's pretty sure what's going on from my description, but he wants to meet with you first. He'll be back next week, and your father and I will drive you down."

I sit up again. "Wait, he didn't say anything about middle child syndrome, did he?"

They look at me oddly, and my mother shakes her head.

"So I have to wait a whole week to find out?"

"You've waited thirteen years, right?" my dad says, closing the door behind them.

"Thirteen and a half," I whisper. By this time Mango has climbed up onto my chest, and I pet him while he purrs loudly. Each mango-colored puff reminds me that even though I'm not dying of a brain tumor, I still don't know what's wrong with me. And my best friend still isn't talking to me. I lie there with Mango for a few more minutes and decide it's time for action.

⬥

Mr. Davis lets me in and tells me Jenna's still up in her room. I knock on the door and wait for her to tell me to come in.

"Oh, it's you," she says. She is standing by her bed, trying valiantly to squeeze her schoolbooks into a purple minibackpack that I haven't seen before. We used to make fun of people with minibackpacks and now she has one. But she's wearing the pajamas I got her last Christmas. I'll take that as a good sign.

"What are you doing here?" she asks.

"Please talk to me." I sit on the bed. "I can't stand it."

She lays down the backpack in defeat. "What do you want me to say?"

For the second time that morning I feel a surge of relief. At least she's not giving me the silent treatment anymore. "I don't want to fight. And I understand why you got mad at me." Then I can't help myself. I mutter, "Even though I really needed you to be there for me."

"That's an apology?" Jenna asks. She crosses her arms in front of her.

I tug at my ponytail for lack of anything better to do while I think of a response. "It's half an apology. The other half has to come from you."

"You're the one who kept the secret," she says pointedly.

I take a deep breath. "Listen, Jenna, I'm sorry I didn't tell you. I just couldn't talk about it. But now I need to talk about it. With *you*. Unless you've got a new best friend I should know about. Like the person who gave you that backpack."

"This stupid thing? A friend of my father's gave it to me. I promised my father I'd wear it at least once."

I'm relieved it wasn't from Kimberly or Molly or Sara trying to move in on my best friend while we were in a fight.

Jenna pulls her clothes out of the closet and lays them on the bed. "I don't want to fight anymore either. But you don't know what it's like finding out something might be wrong with someone you care about. I've been there before, and believe me, it's really scary."

I look down at the floor, ashamed. "I hadn't thought of it that way. I'm really sorry if I made you worry."

"And I'm sorry I got so mean," she says, starting to pace. "But I kind of did a bad thing yesterday after you left school early." Guilt flickers across her face. I recognize it from that time she literally got caught with her hand in the cookie jar. She takes a deep breath. "Well, Kimberly was asking me what was going on with you, and at first I told her I didn't know—because I *didn't* know—but then when I *did* know and I was so mad at you...well, I told her the truth. About you seeing the colors."

"How could you do that?" A dark cloud of dread descends upon me.

"I'm really sorry."

"Who else knows? Wait, if Kimberly knows, then everyone must know!"

"I'm sure not everyone...," Jenna says, trailing off and looking everywhere but at me. I can hear the third-grade laughter ringing in my ears all over again. The passage of time doesn't make it sound any nicer.

"I'd take it back if I could," Jenna insists.

Still stinging from the betrayal, I say coldly, "What's done is done, right? I'm sure eighth-graders aren't as cruel as third-graders." *Yeah, right.*

"No one's going to make fun of you," Jenna says. "They're just curious, that's all."

"We'll see about that."

I hurry out of her house and walk quickly back down the road, suddenly eager to get home. I hate the idea of everybody at school talking about me behind my back.

I'd tried so hard to avoid it, and then Jenna, of all people, sets it off.

Zack is sitting at the kitchen table eating scrambled eggs when I walk in the back door. Seeing him there strikes me as strange. My life is changing by the minute, when for Zack everything is exactly the same as it was yesterday. As I pass by he tosses a handful of salt over his shoulder, spraying me with it.

"Hey!" I say, brushing the tiny crystals off my jacket.

"Sorry," Zack says. "Didn't see you there."

"You better clean that up before Mom sees it. And don't leave it for Mango to lick up."

"Relax," he says and grabs a sponge from the sink. "If you spill salt, you have to throw some over your left shoulder to appease the evil spirits. No big deal."

"The evil *salt spirits?*"

"Go ahead, make fun," Zack says. "But Beth knows it's true."

"You're brainwashing her," I accuse him. "She never used to be this way."

"Hey, the Voodoo Vixen came to me, not the other way around," he says, stuffing a whole piece of toast in his mouth.

I head out of the kitchen, and Zack calls after me in a muffled voice. "By the way, if you can't find Mango, he's probably hiding in the walls."

Like the rest of us, Mango had found the house's little nooks and crannies that never quite fit together. I go back in the kitchen. "Why is he hiding?"

"I think Mom scared him. She was sweeping the hall, and she caught him peeing on the couch. So she chased him with the broom, and I haven't seen him since."

"Mango peed on the couch?" I ask in disbelief.

"Yup. Haven't you noticed he's been a little weird lately?"

"Weird like how?"

Zack shrugs. "Slinking around the house with his tail real low. Sleeping a lot."

"He always sleeps a lot," I snap. "His medication makes him tired." At that minute Mango saunters into the room and heads straight for his food bowl. Zack shrugs.

I bend down and examine him. Poor Mango. Maybe he's suffering from middle cat syndrome and peed to get attention. Being chased with a broom probably wasn't the kind of attention he had been hoping for.

"Five minutes till the bus," Mom yells from upstairs.

I cringe and sit down across from Zack. "Hey, can you show me how you get the thermometer to read like you're sick? I really don't want to go to school today."

"Ah, the ol' thermometer and lightbulb trick," he says fondly. "Never fails. But you only want to use it if you don't mind being brought to the doctor."

I quickly push back the chair and stand. "Ugh, never mind." In my haste I knock over the saltshaker. I turn it upright and pause. With a sigh of defeat, I pour a tiny bit in my hand and throw it over my left shoulder. Salt spirits or no salt spirits, I need all the luck I can get today.

Zack smiles proudly. "Don't worry, I'll clean that up."

I give Mango an extra cat treat, grab my book bag, and head out to the bus stop. Maybe I'm overreacting. Maybe it won't be that bad after all.

Then why do I keep hearing freeeeek, freeeeek, freeeeeeeeeek over and over in my head?

Chapter Six

Throwing the salt must have worked, because no one asks me anything about my colors until English class. That's when the dam breaks. Before the teacher comes in, kids rush over to my desk and begin firing questions at me.

"What color is my name?" Ross Stoler demands. He's never even *spoken* to me before. "How can you read with all those colors floating around?" asks Michelle, the girl with the dirty book. Then the questions come all at once. "Is it true that you can tell the time without looking at a clock? Is it true you can read people's minds? What does it feel like? Does it hurt?"

I turn from one person to the next as the questions get more and more absurd. My face is burning, and I slide down in my chair. Luckily the teacher comes in, and everyone sits down. I catch them glancing back at me when they think I'm not looking. I don't know what they expect to see.

At lunch I suddenly have the most popular table in the cafeteria. I tell people their names are yellow like a ripe banana, sky-after-it-rains blue, burnt-caramel brown, fire-engine red. It's exhausting. Jenna and Kimberly try to protect me by shooing the crowd away. Sara cowers in her seat and silently chews her peanut-butter sandwich. Molly keeps bouncing up and down, clearly loving the attention. I have to admit it isn't *all* bad. Kids who totally ignored me before are clamoring to talk to me now. It would be more rewarding if it didn't have the overtones of a circus sideshow.

"I wouldn't talk so much if I were you," a girl with long blond hair announces as she passes our table. "They might stick you in a class for *special* kids."

I watch her walk away, and my spirits sink with each step. She doesn't even know me.

"Ignore her," Jenna says. "She's just jealous."

After that I don't feel like talking anymore and get a hall pass to go to the bathroom. I hide in a stall until lunch is over.

Just to make the day complete, we have a pop quiz in math. I try hard to focus, but I can't. I wind up leaving the last three answers blank. Afterward we're supposed to start on our homework while the teacher grades the quizzes, but my notebook fills up with doodles instead. The teacher hands the quizzes back, and I leave mine facedown on the desk. I fantasize that I got an A. A nice, happy sunflower-yellow A. Slowly I turn one corner over until a letter starts appearing. It's a big, fat purple F and a note to meet with her as soon as possible.

By the time I board the bus to go home, I'm totally wiped out and in a really bad mood. Someone whispers, "That's her. The girl who sees all the colors." So that's who I am now. The "girl who sees colors." At least they don't know I'm also the girl whose grandfather's soul lives in her cat. They can't take that away from me.

Jenna stayed after school to work on her newspaper editorial about sexism in gym class, so she's not here for me to hide behind. Zack keeps asking me about these rumors he heard about me, but I just stare out the window. He really won't shut up, so when we get home I stand on the front porch and tell him the whole story. He's actually quiet for a change.

"How come me and Beth don't have this?" he asks. "Maybe you're adopted. You don't really look like any of us now that I think about it."

"I'm not adopted," I say, too worn out to argue. "I don't know why I have it. That's why I'm going to all these doctors."

"I think it's pretty neat," he says, following me inside.

"You do?"

"Sure," he says, grinning. "Now I know you're the strangest one in the family after all. And you had some stiff competition!"

I open my mouth to disagree but realize I can't. This is a very sad realization. My father walks in behind us, picking sawdust off his eyebrows. He asks to speak to me alone, but I tell him I already told Zack what's going on.

He seems pleased by that. Dad likes it when we all get along. "Well then, the neurologist's office called. Your appointment is next Friday. It would mean taking you out of school again."

"I think I can handle it."

"Maybe I should come too," Zack suggests. "Mia needs me there."

"When pigs fly," my father says.

"Think that will be any time soon?" Zack asks hopefully.

"Nope," my father and I answer together.

A strange thumping noise brings us to the living room. "That," Zack says, "is not the way the body is supposed to work." Beth is contorted on the floor, her legs above her head with her arms out to the sides. She slowly turns her head and looks at us.

"It's yoga," she says cheerily. "You all should try it."

"Why?" Dad asks.

A hidden voice responds from the other side of the couch. "It clears any blocked energy."

"Mom?" I ask, leaning over to get a better view. Sure enough, there she is, wearing old gardening clothes, bent in some position that looks hard to get out of.

"The Voodoo Vixen's got another one," Zack whispers. "It's only a matter of time till the rest of us are sucked in."

"Not me," Dad and I say at the same time. We smile at each other, and I realize how glad I am to be home.

━

Rain pelts the car as we drive through the university gates on Friday morning. Zack said that if it rains on a really important day, then good things are ahead. At least *something* is ahead, and that's all I can ask. The campus is really nice, kind of medieval-looking with a lot of gray stone buildings and trees everywhere. After a few wrong turns, Dad finds the right building and the nearest visitor parking. We wander up and down the long hallways until we find the right office. My mother knocks on the door, and a tall, sandy-haired man in a white lab coat opens it right away. He barely looks old enough to be a doctor. He reminds me of a movie star, but I can't think of which one. Right away he tells us to call him Jerry instead of Dr. Weiss. His office is small and filled with books of all sorts—fat books, skinny books, old books with pages sticking out, new books still stuffed in bags. I can't imagine that one man could read all these books in a whole lifetime.

"Wow," I can't help saying. "Our town library doesn't even have this many books."

"It's important to keep up with new discoveries in my field," Jerry explains.

"What exactly *is* your field?" my father asks, examining the many diplomas lining the walls.

"As a neurologist, my focus is perception. I study how the brain processes information from our senses and how it relays that information back to the rest of the body." He gestures excitedly for us to sit. "I've studied some unusual cases. As luck would have it, I'm one of the few researchers in the world who has experience with your condition."

My mother doesn't waste any time. "Can you tell us what's wrong with her?"

Jerry smiles gently. "There is nothing wrong with her."

"But something *is* wrong," I insist. "All the shapes and colors with the sounds and the letters and the numbers and—"

"Slow down," Jerry says, still smiling. "Mia, you don't have a disease. You don't even have a problem, exactly. What you have, based on what your mother told me, is a condition that is harmless. It's called synesthesia."

I stare at him for a minute trying to absorb what he just said. Somewhere in my head a chorus of voices sings *hallelujah*. There is a name for what I have! Not that I can pronounce it. "What do I have again?"

He says it again and I repeat it. It sounds like *sin-es-thee-ja*. A gold-flecked word that doesn't exactly roll off the tongue. He explains, "The word *synesthesia* means 'senses coming together.' Imagine that the wires in your brain are crossed, not literally of course. In your case, your visual and hearing senses are linked. The visual cortex in your brain is activated when your auditory cortex is stimulated."

"In *my* case?" I ask. "Do a lot of people have this?" I glance at my parents, who are clearly as surprised as I am.

Jerry shakes his head. "It's very uncommon. We now believe that everyone is born with it, but for most people the extra neural connections are pruned away. For one person in a couple thousand, some of the connections stay. You see, the five senses can cross in many combinations. For instance, I tested one woman who tastes buttered popcorn every time she hears her husband's voice. And there's a well-documented case about a man who feels the sensation of objects being placed in his hands when he tastes certain foods. Seeing colored letters and numbers — lexical synesthesia — is the most common form, followed by colored hearing. Like yourself, forty percent of synesthetes — that's the word for someone with synesthesia — have more than one type."

"Will those other things happen to me too?" I ask, wide-eyed.

"No, you don't have to worry," Jerry assures me. "Your own synesthesia won't vary too much."

"How can we make it go away?" my mother asks. "Mia can't very well walk around seeing colors everywhere. It's interfering with her schoolwork."

"I understand your concern, Mrs. Winchell. Honestly, I do. But this is Mia's normal way of perceiving the world. She can learn to compensate for some things, but we can't 'cure' her. I've never met anyone who wanted their synesthesia to go away."

"I'm still in the room," I remind them.

"Mia," Jerry says, turning to me. "There are some things many synesthetes have in common, besides a slight majority of them being female. Why don't you tell me how many of them sound familiar to you, okay?"

I nod.

"Are you left-handed?"

"Yes."

"Are you artistic? Musical?"

"I paint. I don't play an instrument, but I listen to music a lot. I can always tell what note is being played by its color. If a piano isn't tuned right, I can tell because the colors will be off."

"You're probably a very good speller, right?"

I nod again.

"How do you picture the calendar year?"

"Just like everybody else," I assure him. "You know, like you're sitting on top of a Ferris wheel at the amusement park. January is at the top of the wheel. If the wheel were a clock, January would be twelve. Then as the days go by, the wheel turns to the left, and February is at eleven. By the time summer comes around I'm at the bottom of the wheel, but the wheel is sort of lying flat on the ground now. Then in August it starts to rise again." I lean back, content that at least in this regard I am normal. It takes me a second to register the fact that no one is agreeing with my description. My mother's mouth is actually hanging open.

"Not everyone sees the year like this?" I ask weakly.

The three of them shake their heads. Jerry is smiling. He smiles a lot.

"Do you mean that everyone who has this synesthesia condition has all of these traits?" my mother asks, clearly skeptical.

"Not everyone, of course," Jerry says. "For instance, many people I've tested have problems with understanding math, but on the other hand, one of my former test subjects is now a college math professor. But it's uncanny how many characteristics they do share."

"It's certainly fascinating, Dr. Weiss, er, Jerry," my father says. "But how can we help Mia?"

"Mia can train herself to make different mental connections by narrowing her focus and concentration. It will likely happen automatically as she gets older. Are you sure no one else in your family has this condition? It's often hereditary."

My parents shake their heads. "Will you work with her and see what you can do?" my mother asks.

"Of course," Jerry says. He tells us he has a class to teach now but invites me back the next day to do some tests.

"Are you going to hook me up to any wires?" I ask.

"No wires, I promise." The rain has stopped, and

Jerry walks us all the way out to our car. I'm about to get in when he tells me to wait.

He digs around in his lab-coat pockets and hands me a folded piece of paper. "Here's the address of a synesthesia Web site where you can interact with people from all over the world."

I stare at the paper. "Other people with synesthesia?"

Jerry nods. "All kinds of people with all different types of synesthesia. There are discussion groups you can join and articles to read, although you may find some of them a bit dry."

I'm so excited that I give him a hug. He waves goodbye as we pull out of the parking lot. I settle back in my seat, clutching the piece of paper Jerry gave me. I must find Billy now. I have to let his mother know he doesn't have a brain tumor. He's not crazy. And neither am I.

And the chorus belts out another round of *hallelujah!*

Chapter Seven

By eleven o'clock Saturday morning, Mom and I are sitting in Jerry's lab surrounded by strange machines that hum and beep. I didn't return Jenna's three phone calls last night; I'm just not ready to share what I've learned about myself yet. I almost feel as if she doesn't deserve to know, after what she did. Jerry introduces us to his assistant—a perky graduate student named Debbie, who is wearing rainbow-striped overalls the likes of which I haven't seen since old *Brady Bunch* reruns. She pumps my hand hello and seems very happy to meet me. Jerry asks me about my colors, what shapes I see, what textures, etc. I explain that some letters are shiny, some are gauzy, some are grainy like wood. Some are even fuzzy. Debbie writes everything down.

"How do I compare with other people who have this?" I ask Jerry. "Other synes...synesthetes?" It's still a hard word to say.

"When we first started testing people, we assumed all the synesthetes would see the same colors and shapes for the same sounds," Jerry says. "The initial theory was that if some people, like you, can see a color when they hear a sound, that must mean that the sound actually *has* color but that only a rare few people can see it. But we quickly found that in reality it doesn't happen that way. People's colors seem to be unique to them. The geometric shapes are much more similar. Not that they appear at the same sounds, but the general shapes that synesthetes see don't differ too much. For people who have colored alphabets, there are wide color variations, although many people seem to associate light colors with vowels."

"So to another synesthete my name could be purple with orange stripes when to me it's candy-apple red with a touch of avocado green?"

"Exactly."

I sit back in my chair and let it sink in. My mother just shakes her head, absorbing everything.

Jerry brings us to one of the school's dining halls for lunch, and I suddenly feel very young. And short. I mean, I know I'm short, but I didn't realize I was *this* short.

"Mom," I whisper as we pick up our cardboard trays and get in line, "are all the girls in college this tall?"

Jerry must have heard me, because he starts laughing. "The girls' basketball team practices in the next building, so they come here for lunch. I promise you the other dining halls have shorter students."

I decide that Jerry's kind of cute—for a grown-up, that is. I help myself to a plate of fruit salad and a turkey sandwich. There's no way I can have a crush on Jerry. If he isn't old enough to be my father, he's at least old enough to be my father's younger brother.

We find a table away from the crowd. My mother gives Jerry about a thirty-second head start on his burrito before she begins the onslaught.

"Dr. Weiss, I—," she begins.

He holds up his nonburrito hand. "Jerry."

"Jerry," she corrects herself with a sigh. "I know you said you can't make Mia's condition go away completely. But you can help her work around it, right?"

Jerry turns to me. "Would you want that, Mia?"

He's waiting patiently for an answer, but I can't figure out what to say. I *do* want to be able to pass my classes, and it *would* be nice to be like everyone else. But if I couldn't use my colors, the world would seem so bland—like vanilla ice cream without the gummy bears on top. "I don't know," I admit. "I really *like* gummy bears."

They both look at me questioningly, and I cover my mouth when I realize what I said.

I quickly correct myself. "I mean, I can't imagine life without my colors."

My mother doesn't look too pleased with my response. She picks at her own fruit plate.

"But," I add, "I also don't want to fail my classes."

Mom perks up a bit.

"We have only found a few substances that have any effect whatsoever on the synesthetic response," Jerry tells us. "Stimulants such as coffee and nicotine dampen synesthesia, and depressants such as alcohol can increase it. In order to tell you why that is I'd have to give you a lesson about how the limbic system in your brain functions in response to nerve stimulation."

"I'll take your word for it," I tell him.

"It's also possible for a person's synesthesia to change if something traumatic happens to them. Usually it's dampened until they recover. It may get stronger after early childhood, but it seems to weaken when people approach old age. I can help you work around it, to push it more to the back of your consciousness, if that's really what you want."

My mother looks at me, not bothering to keep her optimistic expression hidden. The only really traumatic thing that I've been through is Grandpa's death.

But I don't remember anything changing with my colors. Maybe it wasn't as traumatic as it could have been because I knew I still had a part of Grandpa in Mango. And we all knew it was coming; he had been sick for months.

"The thing is," I tell them, aware of the quiver in my voice, "my colors help me a lot too. I'm the best speller in my class, and I can remember history really well too. Phone numbers, names, everything. Well, everything except math and foreign languages. But what if I promise to always carry a calculator and to never travel to foreign countries?" I look hopefully at my mother.

Before she can respond, Jerry says, "You don't have to worry, Mia. I truly doubt anything could make your synesthesia disappear forever."

"So what should I do about my problems in school?"

Jerry takes a bite of his chocolate cake and says, "I can set you up with a math tutor in your area. You'll have to arrange your own help with Spanish."

Jerry gives us the tutor's phone number, and we set up the next visit to the university. He walks us out to the car again, but this time I restrain myself from giving him a hug. I don't want to seem like a little kid.

"You seem very happy to know your condition has a

name," my mother says as the car winds through the streets of the campus.

"You have no idea."

"No, I suppose not," she replies, double-checking her map. Then she asks, "He's a nice man, don't you think?"

"Jerry? Yes, I think he's very nice."

"Good-looking, too," she adds, her eyes straight ahead.

"Mom!"

She shrugs and flashes a small smile. "I'm not blind, you know. He looks a little like Paul Newman."

"The salad-dressing guy? No way."

"Maybe it's the eyes," my mother says wistfully as she makes a sharp turn onto the highway entrance ramp. "Those blue, blue eyes."

"I'm telling Dad you have a crush on Jerry."

"I don't have a crush on Jerry," she says. "I have a crush on Paul Newman. *The Sting* was a classic. You kids don't know what you're missing."

I roll my eyes. We argue about Jerry versus Paul Newman for the next ten miles. I have to admit that it's fun being alone with my mother when we're not worried about something.

When we get home I settle down on my bed and force myself to start the homework I've been neglecting. I love the cozy feeling of my bedroom when it starts getting colder outside. I'm feeling very pleased with myself and the world, when Beth walks right in and plops down next to me. She doesn't seem to care that she's crinkling my notebook pages.

"Can I help you?" I ask, pulling my papers out from under her. The coziness is disappearing fast.

"I'm waiting for you to tell me what's been going on," she says, her arms crossed. "I mean, I know the bare bones of it from Zack, but I want to hear it from you."

I glance up at my wall of clocks to see how much time I have before dinner. Mom won't let me check out the synesthesia Web site until after I've finished my homework and we've eaten.

"Can't this wait till later?"

"No problem," Beth says. "I'll just wait right here till you're ready." She leans back on the bed and props herself up with a pillow.

"You're going to wait here? On my bed?"

"Yup. Just pretend I'm not here."

"That'd be a lot easier if you *weren't* here."

"By the way," Beth says, looking down toward the end of the bed, "where's Mango? I was looking for him before."

"Why?"

"I have plans tonight, and I think I'm starting to get a cold. Zack said that if a cat sits on your lap for half an hour, you won't get sick."

I stare at her. "Are you serious?"

She nods.

"Well, he's probably outside."

Beth shakes her head. "Dad said he let him in a few hours ago."

I close my notebook. "All right, you win. Come with me to find Mango, and I'll tell you on the way."

She jumps up and we look around my room. I check under the bed and in the closet, and then we move downstairs. As we open doors and peer under couches I explain about the synesthesia and the doctors. Beth hangs on my every word. It's a little frightening.

We're in the hallway behind the kitchen by the time I finish the story. This section of the house was the last to be "finished," and it's almost totally unusable. The floor slopes slightly downhill, and the hallway is so narrow that Beth and I have to walk single file. At the end of the hall is the tiny room where Mom keeps her telescope and our winter coats. I open the door, even though there's no way Mango could have gotten in there.

"That's some story," Beth says as she pulls the cord to turn on the overhead lightbulb. "Is it true?"

"Of course it's true," I snap at her as I scan the room. All I see are piles of shiny winter coats and snow pants. "Don't make me sorry I told you."

"No," she says quickly. "I'm glad you did. It's really interesting."

I look at her to see if she's teasing me, but there is something that resembles admiration in her eyes. Wow, that's a new one.

Beth glances past me as I try to adjust to this new feeling. "There's your cat," she says, pointing to a stack of gloves and wool hats.

I turn around to see one of Mango's ears sticking out from the middle of the pile. I go over and pick him up. He purrs in my arms. "How did you get in here?" I ask him. He doesn't answer, and this I suppose is a good thing.

I examine the room closely. In one corner the walls don't completely meet. Mango must have traveled between them and somehow wound up here. He seems to enjoy hiding these days. It must be because it's getting colder. I hand him to Beth. "Good luck with the cat cure."

At dinner my father asks if I want to talk about what happened at the lab.

"Not really," I answer, shoving down forkfuls of

lasagna. I burn my tongue on a cheese bubble and swig half a glass of ice water.

"Did they make you run a maze with a big chunk of cheddar at the end?" Zack asks. "Rub your belly and pat your head at the same time? Recite the alphabet backward?"

"That's enough, Zachary," Mom says. "Eat your peas."

I point to my empty plate. "Can I go use the computer now?"

"Did you finish your homework?"

I consider pointing out that it's only Saturday night and that I'd have all day tomorrow to finish it, but I don't want to take the chance. "Yes," I lie, telling myself that at least I feel guilty about lying, and that must count for something. I'll do three good deeds to make up for it.

"How come she gets to leave the table before dinner's over?" Beth complains. "I have plans with Courtney and Brent tonight; can I leave too?"

"Your friends sound like they belong on a soap opera," Zack says. "*Oh, Courtney, your silky hair and milky skin are all I think about! Marry me.*" His laughter forms a pale-blue cloud that kind of drizzles down as it dissolves. I'm fully aware of all my sound-pictures now. Jerry taught me that phrase. *Sound-pictures*. I like it.

"At least I *have* friends," Beth says indignantly.

"We have friends," Zack says. "Don't we, Mia?"

"Not many," I answer as I place my plate in the sink.

Zack sits back and crosses his arms, and Beth glares at both of us. I take the folded Web address out of my pocket and head into my mom's office, where we keep the computer. I close the door behind me.

I log on, type in my password, M-A-N-G-O, and wait for the connection to go through. As soon as it does, I type in the Web address, not even bothering to check my e-mail first. If there is any, it's probably just from Jenna. I wait for the computer to go through all its childproofing so that my site can load. My parents installed so many filters that it's a miracle when anything comes through at all.

WELCOME TO THE WORLD OF SYNESTHESIA! the headline screams out at me as the page slowly loads up. I'm surprised the site isn't more colorful; then I read the first paragraph: "For the consideration of all you synesthetes out there, all the text on this Web site will be printed in black type. Many of you colored-letter folk have complained in the past how frustrating it is to read in a color that doesn't match your own letters, and we aim to please. Remember, one person's green *r* is another person's turquoise!"

I lean back in the chair, amazed. I've learned something about myself after only reading the opening paragraph! Every time I have to read text in colors other than black or white, like in a magazine advertisement or on a book cover, I get a headache because it's the *wrong* color. I try to avoid it whenever possible. Already I feel a sense of belonging with these people. My heart beats faster, and my finger shakes a little as I scroll down the screen. The phone rings next to me, but I ignore it and the red spirals that it causes.

I discover that if I write a profile of myself, it'll go out to other synesthetes who can then e-mail me if they want to. Usually my parents won't let me give out my e-mail address, but I don't think they would mind this time. I put in my name, my e-mail address, my age, and my type of synesthesia, and in the interests and hobbies section, I write "painting, music, being outdoors, and my cat." As I'm about to send it off, my mother walks into the office, so I ask her permission.

She walks over and looks at the screen.

"Go ahead," she says. "Dr. Weiss wouldn't have given it to you if he didn't think it was a safe environment."

"Jerry," I correct her, and wait for her to leave again. She's still here.

"I came in to tell you that a boy from school is on the phone. He wants to talk to you about some history project. How come this is the first I've heard about it?"

I turn around to look at her. "A boy?" I ask. "Roger Carson?"

"Yes, that's his name. He sounded pretty anxious. You better pick it up."

I'd been avoiding Roger and the others in my group. I really don't want to talk to anyone right now, especially about school. "Can't you tell him I'll call him back?"

"I *can*," she says, "but I won't."

I sigh and wait for her to leave before I pick up the phone. "Hi, Roger," I say hurriedly. "Can we talk about this in school on Monday?"

"Did you know we're the only group that hasn't picked a topic yet?" He doesn't give me a chance to answer before continuing. "We have to get together this week. I really need a good grade in history."

While he's talking, I send my profile out to synesthesia cyberspace. I realize he's waiting for me to reply.

"Whenever you want is fine with me," I tell him. "Just let me know."

"How about Monday?" he suggests.

"Fine," I say, half listening as I skim through the titles of the articles I can download. Jerry was right. Most of them are from scholarly journals and have long titles, such as "The Study of Synesthetic Cross-Sensory Modalities as a Result of Various Perceptual Stimuli." If I can't even understand the title, there will be little chance of understanding the article. I suddenly realize Roger is still talking.

"What did you say?" I ask.

"I *said*, we'll meet in the cafeteria at lunchtime and pick a topic. Okay?"

"You want to work during lunch?" I ask, surprised.

"Why not?" Roger asks.

I hadn't sat with anyone other than my friends at lunch since grammar school. And I'd never sat at a table with two boys. I guess if we picked a table all the way in the back, no one would notice. "Nothing. It's fine," I say, trying to sound like I mean it.

I click on an article, see way too many long words, and click on the next one.

I tune back in, and Roger is saying something like "with a list of suggested topics, okay?"

"Sure," I say, not even knowing what I agreed to. I hang up the phone and turn my full attention back to the screen. I read an article about a woman who says she goes to an acupuncture clinic because when the needles go in, amazing colors and shapes appear in front of her face. Another woman says she likes to take a hot bath while listening to music. She says the steam from the bath gives the colors a whole new dimension. About an hour later my eyes are sore and I glance at the phone. When did I say good-bye to Roger? How did the conversation even end? I turn off the computer with a shrug. Whatever it was it couldn't have been too important or else I would remember it. I vow to try that bath thing as soon as possible. Getting stuck with needles isn't quite as appealing.

All those people in their black-and-white worlds— they have no idea what they're missing.

Chapter Eight

First thing Sunday morning I ride my bike to the grocery store. The cashiers are still setting up their registers. I don't see the woman who checked us out the night I met Billy, but she suddenly appears from behind a huge stack of toilet paper. I hurry up to her and tap her on the shoulder. She jumps, and the toilet paper goes flying. I help her stack it back up into a pyramid.

"Sorry about that," I say.

"Can I help you?" she asks wearily.

"Yes, I was in here a few weeks ago. You probably don't remember me, but there was this lady..." I pause, suddenly feeling very stupid. "And her son...he was around five years old, and I was wondering if you might remember them? Their last name is Henkle?"

The woman shakes her head. "You know how many people come in here every day? I'm lucky if I can remember my own name."

"Right," I say, my hopes fading. "Thanks anyway."

Winded from riding home at top speed, I leave my bike on the curb and run inside. It's pretty unlikely that someone would have read my profile already, but I can't wait. I go onto my mail screen, and the message "You've got mail" pops up. I find two letters from Jenna, one from Kimberly, and one from somebody whose e-mail address I don't recognize.

"Please don't let it be some stupid advertisement," I say out loud as I open the mystery letter first.

DEAR MIA,

WELCOME TO THE SYNESTHESIA MAILING LIST! MY NAME IS ADAM DICKSON. I'M FOURTEEN AND IN NINTH GRADE. I LIVE IN BOSTON, AND I HAVE COLORED HEARING AND COLORED NUMBERS AND LETTERS (LIKE YOU) AND I ALSO HAVE COLORED TASTE BUT ONLY A LITTLE. IF YOU WANT TO TALK ABOUT THINGS, E-MAIL ME BACK. OH, I LIKE THE OUTDOORS TOO, AND I ALSO LIKE TO WRITE POETRY, EVEN THOUGH I DON'T TELL ANY OF MY FRIENDS THAT. SO IF WE BECOME FRIENDS, YOU'LL HAVE TO FOR-GET I TOLD YOU. WRITE BACK SOON.

FROM, ADAM

P.S. DO YOU HAVE YOUR OWN COMPUTER? I DO.

"What are you grinning at?" Zack asks as he walks in. His hair is sticking straight up, and he has tooth-paste around his mouth.

"Nothing," I answer happily.

Zack leans over me and peeks at the screen before I have a chance to cover it. "Who's Adam?" he asks. "Your *boyfriend?*"

"Get out, Zack. I'm busy."

"No way. It's my turn to use the computer. You hogged it all last night."

"Isn't there a violent cartoon you can go watch or something?" I ask.

"I'm too old for cartoons."

"Since when?"

"Since right now."

I'm in too good a mood to argue anymore, so I tell him he can use it in ten minutes. He grudgingly agrees, and I'm alone again with my blank reply screen. There are so many things I want to ask Adam, but I don't want to overwhelm him.

DEAR ADAM,

THANKS FOR THE WELCOME. I HAVE TO SHARE THE COMPUTER WITH MY WHOLE FAMILY. IT'S A BUMMER, I KNOW. I'VE ONLY JUST LEARNED THAT MY COLORS DON'T MEAN I'M CRAZY AND THAT I DON'T HAVE SOME AWFUL

DISEASE. I'M LEARNING MORE ABOUT IT FROM DR. JERRY WEISS AT THE UNIVERSITY OF CHICAGO, AND IT'S KINDA COOL. WHEN YOU SAY YOU HAVE COLORED TASTE, DOES THAT MEAN THAT BROCCOLI TASTES LIKE (FOR EXAMPLE) THE COLOR BLUE? OR DOES THE COLOR BLUE TASTE LIKE BROCCOLI? W/B/S (WRITE BACK SOON).

FROM, MIA

P.S. THIS IS THE FIRST E-MAIL I'VE EVER SENT TO A BOY.

P.P.S. I WON'T TELL ANYONE ABOUT THE POETRY.

I send off the letter before I lose my nerve. It's so much easier to talk to people over e-mail than it is in person. I feel like I made a new friend, and I never even left the house! When Grandpa was alive he had a list of like fifty pen pals he met on-line and e-mailed regularly. He met them in different chat rooms, or on card-playing Web sites. He told me once that "youth is wasted on the young" and said it was a shame that other people his age had a fear of computers. When he died my father had to send an e-mail to all of Grandpa's pen pals and tell them the news. I think some of the people still write to my dad. I'm about to open Jenna's letter, when Zack returns and demands his turn. I log off and leave him to whatever mischief he has planned. Once, we got sent a month's supply of nacho-cheese-flavored crackers because of some survey Zack filled out on the Web. They weren't half bad either.

I go up to my room and try to paint, but my mind keeps wandering. Mixing the paint on my palette only makes me think of my colored letters, which make me think of Jerry, which makes me think of my new friend, Adam, which makes me want to check the computer again. I force myself to work on my *Lord of the Flies* book report. Compared to the cruel kids in the book, my classmates suddenly don't seem so bad.

I decide to get some fresh air. Mango must be off hiding someplace again, and this time I don't feel like searching for him. It's a crisp, cool day, exactly as it should be for the beginning of October. There's not a hint of rain in the air, and someone in the valley must have their fireplace going, because I can smell it. My Wild Child instincts take over, and I run across the lawn and jump into a pile of leaves that my dad just finished raking.

"Errooowww!" something screams beneath me, and I hurry to my feet, slipping on the leaves. I wind up back on the ground, landing hard on my butt. I watch the pile of leaves quiver and shake, and out walks Mango, his fur bristling from being sat on. We stare at each other for a minute, and then I gently wrestle him to the ground. When he was a kitten he used to love pretending he was a dog. We'd roll around together, and he'd squeak and meow and then wait for more. After a few minutes I lie on my back, and Mango drapes himself across my chest and starts purring loudly. Fall was Grandpa's favorite season. Maybe that's why Mango's purring so contentedly. I stare up at the bright blue sky and wonder what Adam looks like. I wonder if he wonders what *I* look like. It dawns on me that he could be an old man just pretending to be a fourteen-year-old kid. Now I'm nervous and decide to go back in and write to him again. Mango follows me in the kitchen door, but I lose him to the food dish. Zack is gone. I log on.

DEAR ADAM,

HOW DO I KNOW YOU'RE NOT AN OLD MAN PRETEND-ING TO BE A FOURTEEN-YEAR-OLD KID? I'M GOING TO NEED PROOF.

FROM, MIA

P.S. WHAT COLOR IS MY NAME TO YOU? YOURS IS PALE YELLOW LIKE THE INSIDE OF A GRAPEFRUIT (NOT THE PINK KIND) WITH A TEXTURE KIND OF LIKE GRAPEFRUIT TOO, BUT THE OUTSIDE.

Now, I suppose I could sit here all day and wait for

a letter back. That would be a little too pathetic. But I don't see anything wrong with checking every hour. Or every half hour even. So I manage to occupy myself for the next half hour. I do three math problems (probably incorrectly) and eat a bowl of cereal. When a half hour has passed, I log on again only to find the letters from Jenna and Kimberly that I hadn't read before. I still don't feel like reading them.

Half an hour later. Nothing.

Mom finds me and makes me help her clean out the pantry.

An hour and a half later. Still nothing. I read Jenna's letters. They tell me all the same stuff she already told me last week.

I help Dad wash the helicopter. He lets Zack and me sit in it when we're done. Zack straps himself into the pilot's seat and looks over the gauges as if he knows what he's doing. He asks Dad when he can start flying lessons, and Dad tells him he can take lessons when he's seventeen. Zack in the sky is a very scary thought. While Zack is busying himself by making *vroom*, *vroom* noises, Dad motions for me to step back outside. He tugs at the collar of his flannel shirt. If I didn't know better, I'd swear he was nervous.

"Is everything okay, Dad?"

"I was going to ask you that very question."

"I'm fine," I say quickly. "Why?"

"Do you remember a few summers ago we sent you to that day camp where the swimming instructor wouldn't let you advance from tadpole to guppy?" I nod and wonder if my father's been out in the sun too long.

"Do you remember what I did about it?"

"You marched down there and got me into guppy?"

"Right. Exactly."

He leans casually against the chopper with one hand, and I wait for him to continue. When he doesn't, I ask, "So what's your point?"

"My point," he says, "is simply that I'm here for you. If you need me."

"Thanks, Dad. I'll keep that in mind." I decide not to tell him that I ended up being sent back to tadpole after almost drowning another camper while I flailed around in the deep end.

Two hours later there's still no e-mail from Adam. I'm trying not to be discouraged. I hope my last letter didn't scare him off. Unless he *wasn't* who he said he was after all. I finally read Kimberly's letter. She has a crush on some guy in her gym class. He's only in the seventh grade, but she says he looks much older. She asks me not to tell anyone. I can see that she forwarded the same letter to Molly, Jenna, and Sara, so who else is there to tell?

After dinner I sit down one last time in front of the computer. I try sending out good vibes as the modem dials. Maybe I can ask Beth to cast a spell on Adam to make him write back. I must really be getting desperate.

The vibes must have worked, because there are three letters from him. Three!

Letter number one:

DEAR MIA,

YOU'RE FUNNY. I NEVER THOUGHT I WAS CRAZY, BECAUSE MY MOM HAS COLORED HEARING TOO. I HATE BROCCOLI, SO I NEVER EAT IT. LET'S TAKE CHOCOLATE. IF I'M EATING A PIECE OF CHOCOLATE, I'LL SEE A RECTANGULAR PATCH OF PINK WITH A GREEN STRIPE AT THE BOTTOM. IT JUST APPEARS IN FRONT OF ME AND KIND OF LOOKS LIKE A FLAG WAVING IN THE BREEZE. IF IT'S DARK CHOCOLATE, THE PINK WILL BE ALMOST RED. THIS ONLY HAPPENS WITH A FEW KINDS OF FOOD, BY THE WAY. THE IMAGE FADES AS I KEEP EATING THOUGH. PRETTY WILD STUFF. WE SYNESTHETES HAVE TO STICK TOGETHER — WE'RE THE ONLY ONES WHO REALLY UNDERSTAND EACH OTHER. BY THE WAY, I'VE MET JERRY BEFORE. HE'S NICE.

I PROMISE I'M NOT AN OLD MAN OR EVEN A MAN YET. I GUESS I'M A YOUNG MAN, SINCE WHEN MY MOM IS MAD AT ME SHE ALWAYS GOES, "STOP THAT, YOUNG MAN!" IN

FACT, SHE SAID THAT LAST NIGHT WHEN I MISSED CUR-
FEW FOR THE ZILLIONTH TIME.

— ADAM

He must have a much more exciting life than I do if he misses curfew that often. I think Mom would have a few more choice words for me if I did that.

Letter number two:

DEAR MIA,

WHAT DO YOU LOOK LIKE? DON'T TAKE THAT THE WRONG WAY. I JUST THOUGHT IT WOULD BE EASIER IF I COULD PICTURE YOU. IT DOESN'T MATTER. OH, NEVER MIND, FORGET IT. I'M GOING TO DELETE THIS LETT —

Letter number three:

DEAR MIA,

I MEANT TO DELETE THAT LAST LETTER. PRESSED THE WRONG BUTTON. ARGH. REALLY, IT DOESN'T MATTER WHAT YOU LOOK LIKE. BUT, OKAY, I'LL TELL YOU ABOUT ME. I'M MR. JOE AVERAGE. AVERAGE HEIGHT, AVERAGE WEIGHT, BROWN EYES, AND CURLY DARK HAIR THAT LOOKS REALLY BAD WHEN I WAKE UP IN THE MORNING. BUT YOU CAN PICTURE ME ANY WAY YOU WANT. NOT THAT I'LL DO THAT TO YOU. OH, NEVER MIND!

FROM, ADAM (WHO DOESN'T USUALLY SOUND THIS STUPID)

I'm all jittery and wonder if this is what Kimberly feels like every time she gets a crush on a new boy. Not that I have a crush on Adam. I mean, I don't even know him! But I've never had a boy send me e-mail before. I twist my head to make sure the door to Mom's office is closed, and then I start typing.

DEAR ADAM (WHO DOESN'T SOUND STUPID),

WHERE DO I START? THAT FOOD/COLOR THING SOUNDS REALLY COOL. I'M JEALOUS! MAYBE I'LL KEEP EATING CHOCOLATE UNTIL I START SEEING THINGS TOO! JUST SO YOU CAN PICTURE ME, I ALSO HAVE BROWN HAIR — IT'S WAVY AND KINDA MESSY SOMETIMES, TO BE HONEST. MY EYES ARE GREEN. I'M ON THE SHORT SIDE. MY GRANDFATHER ONCE SAID I WAS SO SKINNY I COULD FIT BETWEEN THE RAINDROPS. BUT THAT WAS A LONG TIME AGO. DO YOU EVER WISH YOU WERE NORMAL? I'M FAILING SCHOOL! WELL, NOT ALL OF IT, BUT ENOUGH!

FROM, MIA (P.S. DO YOU THINK JERRY LOOKS LIKE A YOUNG PAUL NEWMAN? MY MOM DOES!)

I'm shutting down the computer for the night, when Mom walks in with her stern-mom face on.

"What did that boy Roger want last night?" she asks.

"He's in my group for that history project," I say,

hoping that will satisfy her. I try to leave the room, but she doesn't move from the door.

"Exactly which history project is that?" she asks, pursing her lips.

"I told you about it," I insist. "You know, the one about an event in American history that Americans are ashamed of now?"

She shakes her head.

"The one that's half our grade?"

She shakes her head again.

"Oh," I say. "Huh. Well, that's the project. 'Night."

"Not so fast," she says, sticking her arm out in front of me. "You've been very distracted lately. Sometimes I worry the roof could fall on you and you wouldn't even notice. Your math tutor comes in a few days, and you need to be ready. Maybe we should try to find a doctor who can clear this up faster."

I look at her in horror. I couldn't possibly see any more doctors. Especially one who would "clear this up."

"That boy Roger sounded pretty concerned on the phone," she continues. "I hope you're not playing around with the computer instead of—"

"Mom," I interrupt, "I've got it all under control. Don't worry." I push my way past her and head up to my room. I repeat this to myself as I climb the stairs.

Under control. Under control. I pull my art project out from the closet and stare at it. Karen said it showed a good understanding of Kandinsky's style, but that I went overboard in composition. All I did was paint what I saw. I stick it back in the closet and find myself wondering what Adam would think of it. I open my math book and then shut it again. I wonder if Adam likes math.

In the morning, Zack, Jenna, and I shiver as we wait for the school bus.

"I heard there's a new driver this week," Zack announces.

"Great," Jenna moans. "The last time we had a new driver, we didn't get to school until second period."

"And that was a bad thing?" I ask.

"By the way, Mia," Jenna says, rubbing her hands together for warmth. "You were supposed to call me yesterday. I thought we had a"—she glances at Zack and lowers her voice to a whisper—"a PIC mission."

I whisper back, "We did?"

She pulls me aside. "The love potion?" she prompts, then rolls her eyes when she sees I have no idea what she's talking about.

"We were going to take some of your sister's magic stuff and make a love potion for Kimberly!"

"For that seventh-grader she likes?" I ask. "I just read her e-mail about that this weekend."

"We've been talking about it at lunch all week. Haven't you been listening?" I'm about to argue that I did listen, but we both know it would be a lie.

"We'll do it tonight, okay?" I promise her, even though I had been planning on trying out the music-in-the-bathtub experiment. But I don't want Jenna to be any angrier with me.

"I guess so," she mutters. "But you're the one who has to tell Kimberly why we don't have it."

By the time the bus finally lurches to our stop, I'm more than happy to get on it.

Just as I break the news to Kimberly at lunch, I feel a hard tap on my shoulder. I turn around to see Roger. He doesn't look happy.

"Yes?" I say. The rest of my table is watching, except for Sara, who keeps her nose buried in a book as usual.

"We're supposed to be having lunch together," he says, smiling through gritted teeth. Kimberly whistles and Roger's face reddens.

"The history project," he says, "Remember?"

I think for a minute. "I remember there was something I forgot. Does that count?"

He doesn't look amused. "Can we please go work on this now?" He gestures to a table in the last row of the cafeteria. "Everyone else is waiting for you." He turns and sort of shuffles away. I remember he hurt his ankle in gym class last month. See? I don't forget everything.

"I think he's really mad at you," Jenna says.

"Gee, how could you tell?" I ask.

"Even the tips of his ears were red," she replies. "Were you just going to blow him off?" I know she wants to add "Like you blew me off yesterday?"

I toss my half-eaten sandwich into my lunch bag and feel myself starting to get angry. "So what if I was?"

Sara lifts her head from her book. "That's pretty irresponsible, Mia," she says.

"Great," I say, pushing my chair back from the table. "I didn't think any of you would understand what I'm going through. I'm sorry if schoolwork isn't my first priority right now. Or even my second."

I grab my stuff and head toward Roger's table, but not before I hear Kimberly ask Jenna what my problem is. Like *I'm* the one with the problem.

I sit down with my group and give them a half-hearted smile. Nobody smiles back, but at least Roger nods in my direction. Jonah and Laura are in the middle of an argument. I sip my chocolate milk and listen.

"I just don't think dropping the atom bomb qualifies. It was war, after all," Jonah says, pushing his long hair away from his eyes. His hair is so long he could braid it like a girl's. "Plus, besides slavery, everyone's going to choose it."

"So what's wrong with something obvious?" Laura responds, after swallowing a huge forkful of chocolate cake. I can see it stuck in her braces from where I'm sitting. "It would make the research easier, right?"

"I want our project to be unique," Jonah says. "We'll get a better grade that way. How about the Rosenbergs?"

"Who?" Laura asks. I don't know who they are either.

"In the 1950s the government accused them of being spies and executed them," Jonah says, his hair swinging around him as he speaks excitedly. "It was the first time a married couple had been executed. Also something about the first time American citizens were executed for spying in peacetime. It was very controversial."

"Were they really spies?" asks Laura.

"It's possible they were framed," Jonah replies. "I

138

think the government was trying to make an example out of them. It could be the perfect project."

"Wait," Roger says eagerly. "I know what we can do. So does Mia."

I almost choke on my milk. "I do?"

"Remember in fifth grade you did that model of a slave ship for art class?"

"Roger, we already decided against slavery," Jonah says. "What's wrong with the Rosenbergs?"

"Nothing's wrong with them," Roger replies quickly. "But this is a slavery story that I don't think many people know about."

"No one else here knew anything about the Rosenbergs," Jonah mutters into his soda.

"You remember my slave ship after all this time?" I ask.

Roger shrugs. "I thought it was really good. It floated and everything."

I smile at the memory. "Only for about ten seconds. Then it fell apart, and the papier mâché clogged up the drain in the art-room sink for a month."

"What's so unique about a slave ship?" Laura asks. I'm tempted to tell her about the cake in her braces.

"This is a particular slave ship," Roger answers impatiently. "Our art teacher told us about it. Remember, Mia?"

I did remember, what with history being my best subject and all. I sit up straighter now that everyone is expecting something from me. "She told us about this slave ship full of people from West Africa. They called themselves 'Ibos.'" I pause for a second, picturing the colors associated with the date. I translate them back into numbers and come up with 1803. "The ship landed in America in 1803, and the people on board decided they would rather die than become slaves. So they sang a hymn and marched right into the water. Most of them drowned, and the slave traders were really mad."

"So what do you think?" Roger asks, eyeing everyone in turn.

Jonah is the first to speak. "How come we haven't heard about this before?"

Roger shrugs. "I don't know. Maybe you haven't had the right teachers."

"I think it's perfect," Laura says, stabbing her plastic fork into the last chunk of cake.

"Let's do it," Jonah says.

Roger beams at me as if it were all my idea. All I did was remember the story. "Okay then," he says, crumpling up his empty lunch bag. "We can meet next week at my house to divide up the work. Any day except Wednesday—that's when I have acupuncture on my ankle."

I immediately think of the woman I read about on the Web site. She made acupuncture sound so amazing. She said that because of her synesthesia, her senses just came alive. Maybe that could happen for me. We decide to meet at Roger's house after school on Tuesday. I'll have to get Beth to pick me up. I'm sure she'll be thrilled. Laura and Jonah start arguing about how to split up the project, so I decide to ask Roger a few questions.

"Does it hurt?" I ask. "Don't they stick long needles in you?"

"Not only do they stick them in," he says, "but sometimes they twist them around or attach an electrical current to the ends of them. It's a little uncomfortable, but it doesn't really hurt. Why?"

The gears are turning in my brain. If it didn't really hurt, then maybe I should try it. All in the name of research, right? If I could see even a bit of what that woman saw, I could carry that image with me forever, and I bet my paintings would be amazing.

I hear Roger calling my name, but it sounds far away. All I can think of are those colors the woman described.

"Mia!" Roger says loudly, waving his hands in front of my face. "I asked you a question."

Just then the bell rings for next period. I toss my

paper bag in the trash and realize Roger is still standing there.

"Yes?"

"I asked why you wanted to know about the acupuncture."

"No reason," I tell him, making a mental note to come up with a good reason tonight.

"Okay," he says, slinging his book bag over his shoulder and looking away from me. "See you later then." Without waiting for a response, he hobbles out of the cafeteria. I walk to math class alone, wishing the day were already over. I arrive to find a crowd standing in front of the blackboard shaking their heads. The words SURPRISE QUIZ TODAY are written in huge letters. The teacher comes in and announces we have two minutes to review the basic algebra formulas from last week.

My first instinct is to hide in the bathroom, but then I'd definitely fail. If I take the quiz, then I may be able to squeeze by with a D. I hurry to my desk and fling open my math book. Memorizing the formulas was the one thing I totally could have done if only I'd paid attention. I reach into my book bag for a pencil, and my fingers fall on the Magic Markers I use in art class. I pull them out, and an idea forms in my head. I've never cheated on anything before, but I can't fail another math test. It would be too humiliating. And summer school would be too horrible for words. I only have a minute left now, so I quickly pull off the caps on the markers and start drawing a rainbow on my jeans. Only it's not really a rainbow. The colors stand for the letters in the equations. Maroon is x, gray is y, and light blue is z. Yellow is a, brown is b, and red is c. That should do it. All I have to do is put the colors in the right order, and I can tell at a glance what the formula is.

Twenty minutes later the short quiz is over, and the teacher grades them at her desk. We're supposed to be reading ahead in our math books, but I can't help sneaking glances at her. When she's done, she stands up and passes them back to us.

"Excellent, Mia," she says, placing my paper lightly on my desk. She pauses for a second before moving on to the boy behind me.

I finally got my big, beautiful sunflower-yellow A. I'm so proud of myself that I forget to be ashamed.

Chapter Nine

"C'mon, Beth, other people have to use the bathroom too. If we miss the bus, you'll have to drive us to school." I'm banging on the bathroom door while Zack leans listlessly against the wall next to me. "You've been in there for an hour."

"I'm shaving!" she yells out. "Do you want me to cut myself?"

"Do you really want me to answer that?" I reply.

A minute later the door opens, and before I can get in, Zack suddenly springs to life and beats me to it.

"Better work on those reflexes," Beth says as she walks past me, her hair wrapped in a towel.

This is one of those times when being an only child would be really, really good. There's no way I'll have time to shower now, so I might as well check if Adam responded to my e-mail about the acupuncture. I throw on my clothes and hurry downstairs.

DEAR MIA,

THE ACUPUNCTURE SOUNDS GREAT! IF YOU'RE LOOKING
FOR A GOOD FAKE SYMPTOM, ALLOW ME TO SUGGEST AN
EARACHE. THE ONLY THING I'VE EVER DONE TO TRY TO
ENHANCE MY SYNESTHESIA WAS TO GET REALLY DRUNK
ON EGGNOG ONE CHRISTMAS. I LEARNED MY LESSON,
THOUGH, WHEN ALL I SAW FOR THE NEXT FIVE HOURS
WAS THE INSIDE OF THE TOILET BOWL. YOU SHOULD
DEFINITELY GO, NO MATTER WHAT, EVEN IF YOU HAVE
TO SNEAK AROUND BEHIND YOUR PARENTS' BACKS. I CAN
WRITE YOU A FAKE DOCTOR'S NOTE IF YOU WANT.

LEMME KNOW,

ADAM

The fake doctor's note sounds a bit extreme, but
there's no way my parents would let me go if I asked.
I'm very lucky to have Adam to write to, not only
because he's the only one who understands me, but
because I seem to be fighting with everyone in my
family. Just yesterday Zack declared I was acting all
superior because I told him I was too busy to help him
study for his vocabulary test. I told him that maybe,
just maybe, my brain actually was more superior than
his and that my colors are an advancement in evolu-
tion. He said that more likely I'm some kind of a

throwback, and now he's been calling me the Missing Link. I don't think it's very funny.

"Mia," my mother calls out as I'm leaving the small office. "You have a phone call."

I quickly delete the letter, run up to her room, and take the phone. "It's Jerry," she says. I can't imagine what he wants, but I'm just relieved it isn't my math teacher calling to accuse me of cheating. I say hello.

"Hi, Mia. Your mother said you're about to leave for school, so I'll make this fast. The funding just came through to bring a group of synesthetes together over Thanksgiving weekend for a few days of comparing notes. We'll have group discussions, and basically you'll all get to learn from one another. You're one of the lucky ones, since you live only a couple of hours from here. Do you think you'd like to participate?"

My eyes widen. "Definitely!"

"Good. Why don't you put your mother back on the phone, and I'll give her the details?"

"Okay," I say. "Hey, can I bring someone with me who might be a synesthete too? His name's Billy Henkle."

"Of course. Have his parents contact me."

"I don't really know how to reach his parents," I admit.

"But you know his last name, right? Just look in the phone book."

What on earth is wrong with me that I didn't think of that before? I feel like a huge idiot as I hand the phone back to my mother.

"Who's Billy?" Mom asks, holding her hand over the mouthpiece.

"I'll tell you later."

"I can't keep track of your boyfriends," she says.

"Huh?"

She waves me away as she takes down the information from Jerry. While I'm waiting, I pull out the phone book she keeps under her night table. Scanning through the h's, I find no Henkles listed in town, or in the neighboring towns. I try spelling it as many ways as I can think of, but have no luck. I pace across the well-worn carpet until my mother hangs up.

"What boyfriends?" I repeat.

"Don't be embarrassed," she says. "Your brother told me about them."

"What did he tell you?"

"You're going to miss the bus," she says, checking the clock on her night table. "And don't forget you have your math tutor after school."

"Mom, please. I don't have any boyfriends."

"Roger and Adam?" she asks, then chuckles. "You kids grow up so fast these days."

"Roger?" I repeat through gritted teeth. "He's just a

147

kid from school. And I haven't even met Adam in person. I'm going to kill Zack."

I storm out of her room, grab my stuff for school, and walk quickly down the street to the bus stop. Zack must really be mad at me if he made up those things about Roger and Adam. That's something Beth would have done, but not Zack. I didn't even realize he knew Roger's name.

The bus arrives right as I get to the stop. I glare at Zack when I get on and then go sit with Jenna. There's this weird vibe between us now—like we're still best friends, except it's different. I don't know if she notices it or not. Right now she's totally obsessed with planning her party. I try to act as if I'm excited about her selection of decorations, but it's hard. My head is filled with so many more-important things. I was going to tell her about Adam, but she doesn't give me the chance.

Jenna is still talking about the party on the bus ride after school, and I'm actually glad that I have to go straight home for my tutor. As I toss my book bag on the bottom of the staircase, I hear an unfamiliar voice say, "Don't worry, Mrs. Winchell. Mia's going to do great, you'll see."

I tiptoe down the hall and peek my head into the kitchen. My mother is sitting at the table with a girl who looks around eighteen. She has long straight brown hair parted down the middle and sparkly green eyes. She's wearing a wide smile and a low-cut shirt.

"Mia, this is your tutor, Samantha."

"Hi," I say, feeling like a completely different species from this girl.

"Why don't I leave the two of you to get down to work," my mother says, making her exit. "Have fun."

"We will, Mrs. Winchell," Samantha says way too cheerily.

She pushes a chair close to hers and motions for me to sit down. I can see she's already laid out paper, pencils, and textbooks. As Samantha starts talking I begin to wish I were back with Jenna hearing about the party. "Now Mia," she says excitedly, "even though it may not seem like it, math is a concept too. A mathematical equation is asking you to arrive at a number after manipulating other numbers. And the numbers stand for quantities. We're going to teach you to approach math problems differently. In a way, we'll be mapping out the equations in space, until you feel like you can reach out and grab them. Doesn't that sound great?" She is almost giddy.

I wish I could match her enthusiasm, but right now my difficulty with math doesn't seem as important as it used to. And after all, I did get an A on that last test. But Samantha is so eager to help me that I say, "Yeah, that sounds really great," and resign myself to the math lesson. Halfway through it, Zack comes home and barges right into the kitchen.

"Oh, sorry," he says, stopping short and staring at us. "I didn't know you had company."

I sigh. "Samantha, this is my brother, Zack."

"Nice to meet you," she says, holding out her hand.

Zack looks utterly enthralled, and when he takes her hand I'm afraid he's going to kiss it. He hangs around the kitchen for a few more minutes, fixing himself the slowest peanut-butter-and-jelly sandwich in recorded history and keeping one eye on Samantha at all times. Since when did Zack start liking girls?

"Say good-bye, Zack," I finally tell him.

He backs slowly out of the room, still staring and smiling awkwardly. Either Samantha doesn't notice, or she's used to the attention. After two hours she finally runs out of steam, and I feel like I'm going to explode from concentrating so hard. I let her out the front door and go to check out the noises I hear coming from the den. Beth and Zack are both balancing on one foot with their arms held high above their heads. Their eyes are closed.

"Breathe in through your nose, hold it, breathe out through your mouth," Beth says in a low, soothing voice. I watch, mesmerized. Suddenly Zack loses his balance and tips over, almost taking Beth down with him.

Zack looks up at me from the floor. "So what do you think?" he asks. "I look pretty good in this yoga outfit, don't I?"

He's wearing last year's gym shorts and a T-shirt that says "Runs with Scissors" on the front and "Plays Well with Others" on the back. I'm still mad at him for making up the boyfriends thing.

"Actually you look pretty stupid," I say spitefully.

"Missing Link," he mutters as he gets to his feet.

"Jealous much?" I snap back, walking quickly away.

"It's okay, Zack," Beth says, stretching her arms wide. "Don't let her uncenter you with her negativity. Let's go on to the next pose."

The back door opens, and the smell of pizza wafts into the room. Dad must have brought it home for dinner. I run into the kitchen before Beth and Zack can untangle themselves. Dad goes upstairs to get Mom, so for one wonderful second I'm alone with my choice of pizza. Beth and Zack arrive a second later, and each grabs a slice from different boxes.

"I guess yoga makes you hungry," I say.

"You shouldn't knock it till you try it," Beth replies, her mouth already full. "It's very relaxing and centering."

"I'm relaxed and centered enough," I tell her, helping myself to a slice with pepperoni.

"Ha!" Zack says.

"What's your problem lately?" I ask him. "Why did you tell Mom I have two boyfriends?"

"Since when do *you* have two boyfriends?" Beth asks, narrowing her eyes at me.

"Since never," I say, turning back to Zack.

"I told her to get back at you," he says, reaching for another slice already.

"For what?"

"I don't really know."

"Nice."

I hear our parents coming down the stairs, and suddenly I'm not in the mood for a group meal.

"Whatever. Have a great dinner." I put one more slice on my plate and leave the room.

"Where are you going?" Dad asks when I run into him and Mom in the hall. "I haven't seen you all day."

"I'm going up to take a bath since Beth hogged the bathroom this morning," I tell them. "Also, I don't feel so well." That's the truth, in a way. I'm sick of everyone.

"Okay," my father says, sounding a bit disappointed. "Maybe you'll come talk afterward?"

"Maybe," I tell him, climbing the steps two at a time.

I finish the pizza by the time I get to my room, and I lay the plate next to Mango's pill bottle. He raises his head from the bed and gives a sleepy meow. I sit down next to him and scratch under his chin until he purrs like a train engine and mango-colored puffs fill the air. He reaches out a paw and bats at the string on my sweatshirt.

I grab my portable radio, and Mango follows me to the bathroom. He circles the bath mat until he finds the perfect spot to curl up in. He learned the dangers of sitting on the edge of the tub last winter after he fell in and Dad had to blow-dry him. I'm attempting to duplicate the situation the woman wrote about where she saw all the shapes in the steam. I turn on the hot water full blast. Without my Partner in Crime, I'll have to sneak into Beth's room alone to find the last ingredient for my bath experiment. I close the door behind me to keep in the steam, look over my shoulder twice, and then pretend that Jenna is standing guard for me at the top of the stairs. Beth has so many candles that she'll never miss one. I choose a short, squat yellow one from her bookshelf and grab a book of matches from the dresser drawer where I'd seen her stash them. We're all forbidden to keep matches in our rooms since Zack nearly burned his left ear off when he was eight and in his playing-with-fire stage. Beth is supposed to ask one of our parents to light her candles for her. But hey, if she hadn't hidden these matches, I wouldn't have them right now.

I hurry back to the bathroom and am pleased to see a nice hazy mist has developed. The water is almost at the top of the tub, so I leap over Mango and quickly turn the handles. I doubt my parents would be too happy if I flooded the place. I put my clothes into a neat pile, light the candle, and tune the radio to a classical station. I switch off the light and admire the way the candle illuminates the steam. Right away all the colors of the music have more dimension. The steam makes them more solid somehow. It's beautiful! The violins are hundreds of shimmering gold lights, the horns are cubes of green, and the drums are a bright aqua blue. It feels like I can almost reach out and touch them. Eventually I remember I'm supposed to be in the tub, not standing in the middle of the room. The water is really hot, so I get in slowly. The steam is still rising from the water, and I watch the colors flow through it. It's like I'm a part of the whole fabric of the universe—the air, the water, the music, the colors, the shapes, and me right in the middle. I can't believe I'm just discovering this. It makes me want to paint. It makes me want to sing. It reminds me of the sixth-grade field trip to the planetarium. Except this time it's my own personal laser-light show.

Eventually the water gets cold, and since I've already ignored both Zack's and Beth's knocks, I reluctantly drain the water and towel off. As soon as the water is almost gone, Mango jumps into the tub and starts licking the drain.

"That's gross, Mango," I tell him, promptly lifting him back out.

He shakes water off his whiskers, and I swear it looks like he's winking at me. I stash the radio and candle under the sink behind the rolls of toilet paper. As soon as I leave the bathroom Zack rushes in and locks the door. I realize on the way to my room that I haven't done the three good deeds to make up for lying to my mother about my homework the other day. Even though I'm not Catholic, I say a Hail Mary, give Mango his medicine, and then throw in another Hail Mary because I can't think of anything else.

🐭

After a week of stalling, I wake up Sunday morning with one goal—to call Roger and set up the acupuncture session. I can't imagine it could be more intense than the baths, which have become an almost nightly event, and I can't wait to find out. When my clocks read 10:00 A.M. I dial his number. A young girl's voice answers, and I ask for Roger.

"Who's this?" she asks suspiciously.

"It's Mia," I tell her. "I go to school with Roger."

"Roger!" She yells so loud that I jump. "It's your girlfriend, Mia!"

"She's not my girlfriend," Roger hisses in the background. I hear him grab the phone from his sister.

"Sorry about that," he mumbles. I can picture his face turning red. "She lives to drive me crazy."

"It's okay," I say. "She should meet my brother. They have a lot in common."

"So you're calling about the project, right?"

"Uh, r-right," I stammer. "The project."

"Are you having a problem with your part of the research?"

I'm supposed to be researching the religious beliefs of the Ibo people. I haven't even begun, but I can't tell him that.

"I'll have it all done before we meet on Tuesday," I tell him confidently. I shift my internal calendar to Monday night and make a mental note to finish the assignment by then.

Silence on the other end. "So what are you calling about then?"

"We-ell," I say slowly, drawing out the word. "You get your acupuncture on Wednesday afternoons, right?"

"Usually. Why?"

I take a deep breath. "I was wondering if you would let me come with you. I could get the appointment right after yours and then maybe your mom could take me home?" I hold my breath for his response.

After a painfully long pause, he says, "I guess that could work. But why do you need to go?"

Now it's my turn to pause. Before I can respond, he says, "It's okay, you don't have to tell me if it's private or something."

"No, it's okay," I say quickly. "I have an earache that just won't go away." Even to me it sounds like I'm lying.

"Oh," he says. "Well, I'll bring in the phone number tomorrow."

"Can't you call for me?"

"Uh, I guess so."

Relief floods through me. "And your mother? Do you think she can take me home?"

"I don't see why not," he says. "I'll let you know about the appointment as soon as I hear."

I thank him and quickly hang up. I suspect Roger knows I'm lying, and I wonder what he thinks I'm doing it for. He's practically the only person in my grade who hasn't asked me what color his name is. It's actually a deep dark purple, like the skin of an eggplant. We've never spoken about that day at the vet's office either. It's like an unspoken agreement.

Jenna has been asking me to come over for weeks now, so I put on warm clothes and scribble a Post-it note for my parents. I'm just about to stick it on the refrigerator door when voices float in from down the hall.

"I don't care what this Jerry thinks," Dad says, slamming his tool chest closed. "I don't like what's going on."

I stand perfectly still, the paper poised in my hand.

"She's in a phase," my mother answers calmly. "She's just trying to figure out who she is."

"But her grades aren't improving," he points out. "And her report card comes out in a little over a month."

"She recently got an A on a math test," my mother says.

"She did? I didn't know that."

Did I forget to show him the test? I must have.

"It's a little strange though," my mother muses. "That test was before she started working with Samantha."

I don't move a muscle, and I hear them move toward

the front door. My father says something in response, but the furnace kicks in and I can't hear it clearly over the noise. The front door closes and they're gone. My hand shakes as I stick the note on the fridge. I'm half tempted to go back upstairs and lose myself in the bathtub, but I can't risk letting down Jenna again. A phase! Ha! As I open the back door, my friendship bracelet gets caught on the latch and a thread rips. Sucking in my breath, I tuck the broken ends back in place so Jenna won't notice. Maybe we're getting too old to wear them after all.

Chapter Ten

"I thought for sure you'd blow me off," Jenna says as she opens her front door.

"I've never blown you off on purpose," I say, shrugging off my jacket and handing it to her. It's a good thing the pull of the bath wasn't strong enough to keep me away. The awkwardness hangs heavily in the air between us.

"You've been ignoring me," she claims as she tosses my coat into the closet, not bothering to put it on a hanger.

"I'm here now, aren't I?"

"I don't know," she says. "Maybe you're an illusion. Let me see." She reaches out and pinches my arm. Hard.

"Ouch!" I yelp, pulling away.

"Okay, you're real. Dad's making pancakes. Are you hungry?"

"Starved," I say, rubbing my arm. "Then I need to do some research on your computer, okay?"

She stops outside the kitchen. "It's not about the whole colors thing, right?"

"No, it's not," I answer defensively. "It's for my history project. I just don't want to fight with Zack over the computer."

"Okay then," she says. In the kitchen Mr. Davis is flipping his special blueberry pancakes. I stop short when I see an unfamiliar woman sitting at the table. I know it can't be a relative because I've met them all.

"Mia," Jenna says in a formal voice, "this is Rebecca. A friend of my father's."

I try not to show my surprise.

"Nice to meet you," I say stiffly.

"Same here," Rebecca replies in a throaty voice. I think it's supposed to sound sexy, but it just sounds like she's all stuffed up. And who wears a full face of makeup on a Sunday morning? She must be the giver of the purple minibackpack.

No one says anything after that. Jenna's dad breaks the silence with, "So, Mia, ready for my world-famous flapjacks?"

"Uh, sure," I answer, choosing a seat across from Rebecca. I keep glancing at Jenna, but she's shoveling forkfuls of pancake into her mouth as if she hasn't eaten in a week.

"We haven't seen you around here in a while, Mia," he says, neatly sliding a pancake from the frying pan onto my plate. "Got a new boyfriend?"

"Dad!" Jenna moans.

"No!" I vehemently deny. Rebecca smiles a little half smile that suggests she thinks I'm lying, and I decide I definitely don't like her.

"I know," he says, joining us at the table. "You were recruited by the CIA and have been out of the country on a secret mission."

I shake my head again and dig into my breakfast, matching Jenna bite for bite.

"Abducted by aliens?"

"Nope," I answer with my mouth full and my eyes focused on my plate.

"I'm just teasing you," he says finally. "I know what you've been doing; Jenna told me a few weeks ago."

"Oh," I say, looking at Jenna. She keeps eating. She's going to choke if she doesn't slow down.

We continue eating in silence for a minute, until Rebecca asks us what we're planning on doing today. I'm about to answer her when Jenna hops up from the table and says, "Nothing special. C'mon, Mia, let's go."

Mr. Davis and Rebecca share a look. Jenna's halfway out of the kitchen before I catch up with her.

"That was rude," I whisper as we climb the stairs to her room.

"So what?" she says. "Sundays are supposed to be family time, you being considered family of course. She shouldn't come over on a Sunday morning. She's the rude one if you ask me."

We lie down on Jenna's bed, and she changes the subject. "So what's been going on with you lately? You're in your own world most of the time."

I'm about to point out that all *she* seems to care about lately is her party. But I don't want to fight again. If she really wants to know what's going on with me, then I'm going to tell her. The floodgates open. I tell her about Adam's e-mails and the whole acupuncture thing. I even tell her about my baths and about the upcoming meeting. She listens patiently but stares at the ceiling the whole time.

After a minute she says, "Wow, you've been busy."

"So what do you think?" I ask, leaning up on my elbow. "Isn't it cool?"

"Yeah, it sounds cool. I still don't really understand it though."

"Right," I say, pulling at the loose strings on her flowered comforter. "Sorry."

"Do you think it's something I could learn?" she asks, moving her pillow so she can sit up. "I remember things really well. I'm sure I can memorize the color of each letter."

"It doesn't work that way," I tell her, trying to keep my voice even. "It's something you're born with."

"So you were born with it and I wasn't." After another long pause, she asks, "When is this big meeting you're going to?"

"The weekend after Thanksgiving."

She jumps off the bed. "But my party's that Saturday night!"

"I know," I say quickly, hoping she couldn't tell I had actually forgotten. Maybe I *am* a bad friend! "The meeting will be over in the afternoon. I'll be back in plenty of time."

"And you'll help me set up?"

"Of course!"

She hands me a pen and paper from her desk. "Good. Let's work on the list."

I have only written down six names when Jenna's father knocks on the door and asks her to come downstairs.

"Why?" she calls out.

"It will only take a minute," he says firmly.

She grunts and takes her time getting to the door. I move over to her computer desk and log on to the Internet. A whole list of references pops up for Ibo, and I print them out to look at later. Homework on a Sunday should be illegal.

Jenna comes back in and slams the door behind her.

"Uh-oh," I say. Before these last few months I'd never seen Jenna get mad. Even when her mom died, she seemed really sad, not angry. I would have been so angry at the world, but that's just not Jenna's personality. At least it didn't used to be.

"You have to be nicer to Rebecca," Jenna says, imitating her dad's voice. "Rebecca feels bad you don't like her," she continues. "Like I care how Rebecca feels!" She falls back onto the bed, and tears of frustration slide down her cheeks. I sit next to her and stroke her arm.

"Why haven't you told me about her?" I ask. "How long has she been around?"

Jenna sniffles. "About six weeks, I guess. I didn't tell you because I kept hoping she'd go away. Things were fine without her."

"This is just his first girlfriend," I point out. "It doesn't mean he's going to marry her."

"He better not," she says, sounding horrified.

I pick up the birthday list. "Let's keep going. Do you want to invite that girl from your gym class who refuses to wear her gym uniform because she thinks it's un-American?"

"I don't care," she says in a flat tone.

"But you like her."

"I don't care about the stupid party," she snaps, grabbing the paper from me and tossing it in the air. "Maybe you should just go home."

"Why?"

"I want to be alone."

"Are you sure?" I ask. "We can go on a PIC mission and melt all the makeup in Rebecca's pocketbook. The stove top's probably still warm enough."

"Tempting, but not today," she replies, holding her bedroom door open for me. I grab my computer printouts and hurry after her. She already has my jacket in her hand by the time I reach the bottom of the stairs.

The first time in weeks I go to see her and she throws me out. "I'll see you at the bus stop tomorrow, okay, Jenna?"

She nods miserably and closes the door behind me. Before I get more than a step away, Jenna opens the door again.

"Wait," she says. "Do you think your mom could give me my mother's birthday present early this year?"

She looks so small and sad standing in the big wooden doorway. I just want to give her a hug and tell her everything will be all right.

"I'll ask her," I promise.

"You know what?" she says. "Don't bother."

"Are you sure?"

"Yes," she says, and closes the door for good this time. I stand there for a moment longer and then walk home slowly.

Everyone is out when I get home, and the house seems very quiet. At least I can't fight with anyone if I'm all alone. I settle into Mom's office and look up the Ibo references on the Internet. I learn that they are also called Igbos, and that they believed that after their death, the gods would return their souls to Africa. That's why they drowned themselves—to go home.

The phone rings and startles me. I drag myself away from the Ibos and answer it.

"Is Mia there?" a boy's voice asks.

"This is Mia," I respond tentatively, searching my brain to match the voice to anyone I know.

"It's Adam."

"Adam?" I ask, sitting straight up in my chair. "How did you get my number?"

"Dr. Weiss, I mean Jerry, gave it to me. I hope you don't mind."

"No, I don't mind," I answer. My hand holding the phone is rapidly becoming sweaty. "Why were you talking to Jerry?"

"He called and invited me to the big meeting out there."

"But you live all the way in Boston."

"I know," Adam says, excitement coating his words. "But we've worked together before, and he knows I have relatives out there I can stay with. We'll finally get to meet each other."

I suddenly feel shy. "Looks like it."

Just then, someone else picks up the phone. I know it's not at my house since I'm home alone. It better *not* be at my house since I'm home alone! Images from every scary movie I've ever seen run through my head, and my hand almost drops the phone.

"I need to make a call, Adam," a woman's voice says, much to my relief. My heart rate slows back to normal.

"Just a second, Mom." We wait to hear the click before we resume talking. "So I guess I'll see you in a few weeks."

"I guess so," I reply, wishing I could come up with something more intelligent to say.

We hang up, and I jump out of the chair like my feet have springs. I suddenly feel this need to celebrate by hugging Mango. I search through the house, but he's doing a good job hiding. He finally resurfaces right before bedtime. He must have had a busy day getting his revenge on the squirrels because he's very tired. Every year when it starts to get cold, the squirrels come out in full force to make sure the nuts they buried over the summer are secure. Last year at this time, Mango was smaller than the squirrels were, and they used to chase him all around the backyard. I bet this year he's letting them know who's really the boss of the yard. I try to entertain him with his stuffed Tweety, but he just rolls over and purrs. He swallows his pill without even chewing and settles down for the night on my pillow instead of on his blanket. His mango-colored wheezing keeps me awake, and finally I have to move him to his usual spot at the foot of the bed.

When my alarm goes off in the morning, I awake to find Mango sitting on the window ledge, no doubt planning his next attack. Before I can roll out of bed, Zack pushes my door open and sticks his head in.

"So? How do I look?"

"Huh?"

"My ears!" he says, turning his head from side to side

"Oh, right. It's Halloween! They look good. Very natural." Zack has dressed up like Spock each year since he was six. I keep telling him no one watches the original *Star Trek* anymore, but he won't listen. Thankfully he's outgrown the rest of his costume, so this year he's only wearing the ears. I remember when Halloween was my favorite holiday. Now I had forgotten all about it. I guess I'm growing up.

At breakfast I figure I better try to be sociable so my father doesn't worry so much. I tell him I think Mango is chasing the squirrels this year.

"I don't want to clean up any squirrel carcasses," he says, biting into his toast with homemade apple jam. He is oblivious both to the falling crumbs and to my mother's glare as she sweeps them into her hand.

"Mango doesn't actually kill them," Zack says, his arm stuck halfway into a cereal box. "He just scares them and chases them up trees."

"Cats can climb trees," Dad reminds him.

"Remember the last time Mango climbed a tree?" I ask.

"I remember," Mom says. "I think the fire department is still laughing to this day."

"What was it exactly that they said?" Zack asks her, even though he knows very well. It's a story he never gets tired of hearing.

"They told me, 'Hey Lady, have you ever seen a cat skeleton in a tree?'"

The three of them dissolve into laughter, but that was an important day for me. When Mango finally made his way down that tree, sliding on the slippery bark, he was scared and shivering. Still not fully grown, he snuggled into the folds of my sweater, and I petted him until he calmed down. That was the first time I knew he needed me.

Breakfast is over when Beth comes in and starts yelling that Mom washed her white sweater with her red sweater and it's now a pink sweater and what is she supposed to wear to school?

"You could wear a Halloween costume," Zack suggests. "I have some extra ears."

"Mom!" Beth wails.

"Live long and prosper," Zack tells Beth before we run to make the bus. She is not amused.

That afternoon I arrive at history class before Roger. I wait outside the door, impatiently tapping my fingers against a cold metal locker. If he doesn't hurry, the bell is going to ring.

Mrs. Morris walks past me into the room. "Are you joining us, Miss Winchell?"

I have no choice but to follow her in. Just as the bell rings, Roger ducks into the door and slips into his seat. I stare at the back of his head, willing him to turn around. He's too far away for me to whisper to him, and the last time somebody was caught passing a note, Mrs. Morris tacked it up on the bulletin board.

After the longest fifty-two minutes I can remember,

I corner Roger at his desk before he can even stand up. I'm about to pounce, when he holds up his hand to stop me.

"Before you ask, the answer is yes. My mother set up the appointment for after school on Wednesday. She's going to call your mother tonight."

"Oh, she is?" I say nonchalantly.

"That's okay, right?" he asks as we leave the room together. "She does know about this, doesn't she?"

"Of course she knows," I reply. "Well, she kind of knows." Then, "Okay, no, she doesn't know."

"Why haven't you told her?"

"Um, she doesn't believe in acupuncture?"

Roger looks at me sideways as we walk down the hall. "Why haven't you really told her?"

I stop walking. "Listen, you said if it was private, I didn't have to talk about it, remember? Can't you just tell your mother I have permission?"

"I guess so," Roger says, clearly not pleased. "But how are you going to pay for it then?"

I hadn't thought of that. "I have some money saved," I tell him, "from allowance and odd jobs and stuff."

"Okay," he says. "If it's that important to you."

"It is," I tell him as forcefully as I can muster. I'm about to thank him, but he hobbles off before I get a chance.

We have another test in math class today. I suppose I could try to use the methods Samantha taught me, but that seems more trouble than it's worth. After all, I'm already prepared with the markers, and it hardly feels like cheating anymore. I use the bottom of my sneaker this time since I'm not wearing jeans today.

When I get home Mom is setting up her telescope in the front yard. There's some big planetary-alignment thing tonight that she's been talking about for weeks. I intend to stay on her good side for a while. Then maybe she won't ask me why I'm not coming home after school on Wednesday.

"Mia, I'm hoping you'll get dinner ready for me tonight so I can work out here. I already made the salad, you'd just have to put up the pasta."

"Sure, Mom," I say. "No problem." I step around her and head to the front door.

"Oh, Mia," she says, her back to me. "How was the math test today?"

I stop with my hand on the doorknob. "It was good," I tell her, holding my breath.

"Great," she says. "I'm proud of you."

I wait until the door is shut behind me to breathe again. My plan is to lie low for the rest of the afternoon. Since Mom is outside, she won't need me to hand out the candy to the trick-or-treaters. I work on my Ibo report and peek out the window at all the little witches and firemen and brides and monsters. They have no idea how complicated life can be. At six o'clock I make dinner. Nobody thanks me. They all eat in a hurry and then go outside to watch Mom watch the stars. No one helps me clean up. I wring out the sponge over the sink and keep repeating one thought in my head: *Wednesday cannot come fast enough.*

Roger lives right near the school, and on Tuesday the four of us walk to his house together. Roger leads us into the kitchen and tells us to set up camp at the round wooden table.

"Oh, do you have a dog?" Laura asks, almost tripping over a big silver doggie bowl. Right next to it is a squeaky toy in the shape of a steak. "Because I'm allergic to animals with fur. I get hives all over my arms and legs."

Roger slowly closes the refrigerator and sets down four cans of soda. He shakes his head. "No, we don't have a dog, so you don't have to worry."

Laura glances at the bowl on the floor and then looks questioningly at me. I guess Roger's family isn't ready to let go yet. I can't meet Roger's eyes until the meeting is half over. After a while no one has anything left to say about the Ibos, so we move into the den and watch videos. Beth picks me up at five o'clock. Her friend Courtney is with her, so I have to sit in the back. The two of them ignore me and blabber on about what they're going to wear to the junior prom, which is something like seven whole months away. I'm glad they're not talking to me so I don't have to pretend to care about their dresses. For dinner we have the left-overs from the meal I cooked yesterday, and again, nobody thanks me.

I'm already out of my seat when the final school bell rings on Wednesday. Roger is waiting for me by my locker as planned, looking uncomfortable. I toss my books inside and grab my backpack. He had told me to wear comfortable clothes, so I'm wearing the loosest pants and sweater I could find. I feel like I'm in my pajamas.

I climb into the Carsons' minivan and notice that it still smells faintly of dog. Roger and I don't say much on the way to the acupuncturist, which is fine because Mrs. Carson talks enough for everyone. All that's required of me is an occasional "Oh?" and "Uh-huh."

She lets us off in front of the office and then goes to park. A little bell rings as we open the door, and the waiting room is very warm and inviting. I recognize the smell of vanilla incense because Beth's been burning it recently. There's a chart on the wall showing the points where the needles go in. I start to feel a little faint.

"I'm supposed to go right in," Roger says. "You need to sit down and fill out a form." He points to a clipboard on the unoccupied front desk.

"Okay," I tell him, reaching for it. He heads into one of the open office doors, and I remain standing in the middle of the room.

"You all right?" he asks, turning slightly.

"Uh-huh," I reply. "I'm fine."

"It doesn't hurt," he says. "You don't have to worry."

"I'm not worried."

"Then why haven't you moved from that spot?"

"No reason."

Just then, the doctor comes out from the back and ushers Roger into the room. She is around sixty years old and looks a lot like my last memory of Grams. This makes me feel a little better. After all, Grams would never hurt me.

The door closes behind them, and for a second I'm alone in the office. For that second I seriously consider leaving. Maybe this is a bad idea. Then Mrs. Carson enters from outside, complaining that there's not enough parking in this one-horse town. The cool breeze from outside wakes me up a little. I sit down and begin filling out the form. It would take me an hour to answer all these questions. I skip down to the bottom where it asks why I'm here. "Earache. Both ears." Mrs. Carson quietly flips through the pages of some kind of alternative-healing magazine. She can't possibly read anything that quickly. After about fifteen minutes, Roger comes out of the office, limping slightly less than before.

"Your turn," Roger says.

I smile weakly and give him my seat. I walk over to the office door and peek in. The room is very small, with a long padded table in the center and shelves along the walls.

"Come in, come in," the acupuncturist says with a wave. "I won't bite."

I step in the room and close the door behind me. "I'm sorry. I'm not very good around doctors, I guess."

She pats the table next to her, and I sit on the edge of it. "My name is Faith, and if it makes you feel any better, I'm not a real doctor."

I look up with a start. "You're not?"

She shakes her head and talks to me while she looks over my chart. "I am certified in the practice of acupuncture. You know how doctors study anatomy so they know how the body works?"

I nod.

"It's very similar. I know where all the energy centers of the body intersect, and I can tell when they're not flowing properly. That's how I know where to put the needles in and how to rotate them. Do you understand?"

I tell her I do, even though it all sounds pretty bizarre. All the talk about energy flow reminds me of Beth's yoga stuff. I can't believe I'm doing something that Beth might agree with! Faith directs me to lie down and tells me that for our first session she's only going to leave the needles in for ten minutes. I close my eyes so I can't see what they look like.

"That's good," she says gently. "Close your eyes and relax. Have faith in Faith." She laughs at her joke, and I try to smile but I'm too nervous. My lips just twitch.

"Can you describe the earaches?"

My heart sinks. I hadn't thought of this part. "Um, just a general ache in the middle of both ears. Usually just in the morning." I'm going to have to do more than three good deeds for this one!

She nods thoughtfully. "I'm only going to use six

needles on you today. Two will go at your ankles, two at your hips, and two in your upper ears."

Just as I wonder what the heck I'm doing here and how I can make a graceful exit, I feel a pinch on my left ankle, then my right. But the pinches don't go away, and I open my eyes slightly and look down. There are long needles sticking out of my ankles! Now she's at my hip, and I squeeze my eyes shut again.

"How come I'm not bleeding?" I ask as the needles go in my hips. I try not to picture what they look like.

"The holes are so small that when I pull the needles out, the skin closes up before any blood can come out. Sometimes you might get a little bruise or a few drops of blood if I hit a small vein." She must be used to answering that question. "But that's not likely."

I'm beginning to feel a little woozy. Tiny gray balls float in front of my eyes. Faith moves the hair away from my right ear, and I can actually hear the needle penetrating the cartilage. The tiny gray balls turn silver, bright silver, and now there are swirls of yellow mixed in. The needle goes in my other earlobe, and small bubbles, like multicolored marbles, enter from the left and zoom in front of my face until I lose sight of them. I've never seen colored shapes before without sounds triggering them. I can't believe I can do this!

The bubbles are now undulating and forming the most incredible streaks of color.

"Ohhh," I squeak, unable to keep it in. "Wow..."

"Is everything all right?" she asks.

I try to answer but can't tear my focus away from the visions. Faith's voice sounds very far away. "Uh-huh," I somehow manage to respond. I force myself to stop smiling so she doesn't think I'm a loon. The woman who wrote the article described seeing the bubbles, but her description didn't do it justice. She must not have seen what I'm seeing.

"If you're okay with this, then next time I'll use the electric current with the needles."

I nod, still vaguely aware of the pinching in the same way that I'm vaguely aware that I'm not alone in the room. All that matters is the display before me.

Then suddenly it's gone. Faith pulls out the last needle and rubs the spots with a little ointment. I open my eyes but don't move. I feel like I just awoke from some amazing dream.

"You can lie here for a few minutes if you like," she offers. "Your *chi* was activated, and you'll need to release it slowly."

"My what was what?" I ask, still staring up at the ceiling.

"Your *chi*," she repeats, "was turned on. Chi is the

Chinese word for our internal energy. The acupuncture needles direct it around your body to help you heal."

I'm about to ask her how soon I can come back when I notice there is an indistinct brownish-pink cloud around her upper body. I glance at the ceiling, then back at her. It's still there. I sit up and rub my eyes. She moves across the room to open the door, and the haze goes with her, but it also trails behind. I can still see a brownish-pink glow where she was first standing.

I force myself to get off the table and follow her and her trailing cloud into the waiting room. Roger and his mom look up. Roger is encased in a tomato-red glow, and his mother is yellow. Since Roger is a purple name, it is very unnerving to see him in red.

I try not to stare at everyone while I wait for Faith to tell me how long it will take until my chi settles back down again.

"Everyone's different," she says, sticking my chart on a crowded shelf. "Probably a few hours."

Roger joins me at the desk, and we schedule our appointments for next week. I can't help watching the red haze swirl slightly around his head. Tiny tendrils float away from him as he talks to me. As we walk to the car I look closely at the people passing us. Everyone has their own misty aura around them. Some people's auras are very active, with tendrils and balls shooting off of them and landing on other people. How are those people doing that? How come nobody notices this? My legs feel like rubber, and I'm on the verge of totally freaking out.

In the confined space of the car the color clouds are brighter. They seem to fill all the available space. From the passenger seat, Roger asks me what I thought of my session. His voice sounds muffled, as if it's buried under layers of red.

"It was amazing," I tell him, my voice cracking. "Thank you so much for bringing me."

"It was amazing?" he asks, not hiding the surprise from his voice.

Oops. "I mean, it was fine." I lower my voice to a whisper. "Roger, do you ever see anything afterward? In the air?"

"No," he says. "Like what?"

So it's just me after all. "Never mind. Thanks again for bringing me."

"No problem." He turns to face the window. I can see in the reflection of the glass that he's blushing. His cloud grows brighter and shimmers for a few seconds. I stare in awe as a long tendril winds itself off of him, lands on my shoulder, and instantly disappears into my own green haze. I look down at myself. My own green haze! I have it too! I hadn't thought of that. A feeling of jubilation spreads through me. I am seeing invisible things!

Beth's friend Brent's new red sports car is in our driveway, so Mrs. Carson lets me off at the curb. Most people who live out here have trucks since some of these roads can be pretty bumpy. Maybe Brent thinks a sports car matches his soap-opera name. Beth can't stop talking about the car, even though she and Brent are "just friends."

I thank both Mrs. Carson and Roger again, profusely, and practically skip across the lawn. Beth and Brent walk out the front door while I'm still a few yards away. I duck behind the big oak tree and watch them. Beth's yellowish-brown glow is very similar to Brent's golden-brown one. Brent says something to Beth in a teasing voice, and her colors glow even brighter and do a shimmering little dance like Roger's had done in the car. I couldn't hear what Brent said, but Beth must have liked it. Tiny tendrils break off from her color cloud and blend with his. My heart beats faster as I watch this. I feel like I'm watching a science-fiction movie. I get the very real feeling that Beth and Brent are most definitely more than friends! They get into Brent's car and pull away, never noticing me. I'm happy for her. I'm happy for everyone and everything—all the creatures on the planet. Adam is not going to believe this!

I skip into the house feeling like I'm magic. I step right over Zack, who's sitting in the hallway surrounded by his ever-expanding comic collection. His silver cloud twinkles happily. Mango slides across the freshly waxed front hallway and leaves a mango-colored streak behind him. A wonderful magical mango streak that fills my heart to bursting.

Chapter Eleven

The first thing I do when I wake up in the morning is lift up the covers and stare down at my legs. No more green glow, just crumpled baby-blue pajamas. I flip over and bury my face in the pillow. My new powers lasted until I went to sleep, and that was really late because I was up watching my family's clouds interact with one another. I could tell that when my mother agreed to host my dad's poker game at the house, she didn't really want to. But I could also tell how grateful Dad was. I could tell that when Zack said he finished his homework, he really had done it. And when Beth said she was at the library all afternoon, I knew she wasn't. But I knew that the old-fashioned way — by spying from behind a tree. No one even asked me where I was after school.

Mango nudges my ear and forces me to flip back over. I miss the bright mango glow around him and rub him until he purrs. Ah, there they are, his usual small mango-colored puffs. *Today is Thursday*, I tell myself as I brush my teeth. That's one day closer to when I can go back to the acupuncturist. Just six more days. I stop brushing and multiply twenty-four times six in my head using the process Samantha taught me. One hundred forty-four hours! That is not good! Something must be done. As I hop in the shower it occurs to me that a few weeks ago I would have been ecstatic to have multiplied numbers in my head. I guess life is all about priorities.

Right before homeroom I corner Roger by his locker and ask him if we can get earlier appointments, like for this afternoon. He says no and gives me some lame excuse, like Faith works in another office on the other days of the week. I notice as he walks away that his limp is getting better. I might have to kick him so he'll keep needing the acupuncture.

In history class we break up into our groups. I hand each of my group members a copy of my cleanly typed research paper and collect theirs in return. Someone has to combine our four papers into one report, and it isn't going to be me. I've done my share. I lean back in my seat and fold my arms.

"I think we need something more than just a written report," Jonah says, tapping his pencil on the plastic desk to some inner beat. "How about we make a scale model of the ship? Mia, you're the artist, right?"

"Huh?" I untangle my arms. Can't they tell my role in this is finished?

"C'mon, Mia," Roger coaxes. "We'll worry about the written part if you make a model of the ship. Or a painting even!"

"But I already did all that research," I tell them, aware of the whine in my voice. "Now you're saying I could have painted a picture all along?"

Jonah waves my papers in the air. "You only wrote a page and a half!"

"That's all the information there was on the Ibo religion," I insist. "Honestly."

"Just do the painting," Laura snaps at me. "If I could paint, I would do it myself."

"Fine," I tell them so they'll leave me alone.

"Make sure you write it down so you'll remember," Jonah says. "We present the project the day before Thanksgiving."

When we go back to our regular desks I make a big show of adding the task to my homework list. At least if I'm busy painting, then the week will fly by faster. It's been a while since I've painted anything that wasn't an art-class assignment.

In Spanish the teacher hands back our in-class essays

from the day before. I got a C minus, which, pathetically enough, I'm happy with.

When Zack and I get home from school we find a note stuck on the front door in Mom's handwriting: "Tonight is the food drive at the elementary school. Everyone be home by 6:30. McDonald's on the way there. Wear sneakers. NO EXCUSES." Every year around this time we put boxes of Thanksgiving food together for the people in town who can't afford it. Some of the extra boxes go to a homeless shelter in Chicago. The food drive takes place in the gym at my old elementary school, and we've gone for the last three years. Any activity to pass time faster is fine with me. Plus this will cover me in the good-deeds department.

"Good," Zack says, pushing open the door. "Another hamburger for the scoreboard. It's been too long."

"You were just there last week for that kid's birthday party."

"You're right!" he says, slapping his forehead dramatically. "I forgot to enter that one!" He throws his jacket in the hall closet before bounding up the stairs to his room.

"Aren't you getting a little old for birthday parties at McDonald's?" I ask as I pass his room.

He's too busy filling in the date of his missed burger to answer. I sit down at my desk and search through the piles of Ibo books for a good picture of the ship. I have the picture picked out and tacked up to my canvas when Dad yells upstairs that it's time to go.

"Where's Beth?" I ask as I slide into Dad's backseat next to Zack.

"She had a prior engagement," Zack says, perfectly imitating Mom's voice.

Mom throws him a look from the front. "She has a school project she has to finish."

"So do I," I say. "What happened to 'no excuses'?"

"Beth's grades are more important than ours," Zack says.

"That's not true," Mom insists. "But she's working toward college now."

We pull out of the driveway and head into town.

"I bet she's out with Brent anyway," I whisper to Zack.

"Oh, I'm sorry," Zack says innocently. "Are you talking to me again? It's been so long since you've said anything nice."

"Never mind, Yoga Boy." I turn toward the window.

"Missing Link."

"Dork."

"Don't make me pull over," Dad threatens good-naturedly.

Zack leans over and whispers, "What do you know about Beth and Brent?"

"Plenty, but now I'm not telling."

"I'll find out anyway," he says. "Just like I found out about your boyfriends."

"Don't make me hurt you," I warn him as the golden arches of McDonald's come into view.

Zack dances out of the car singing, "*One hundred twenty-six, here I come!*"

My mother makes us scarf down our food in four minutes, reinforcing the definition of *fast food*. By the time we arrive at the school gym, it's crowded with families. I force myself to tune out the noise so the colors don't overwhelm me. Not an easy feat, but I can do it if I concentrate. My family splits up. Dad heads over to the frozen-turkeys area, Mom goes to the distribution tables, and Zack and I join the kids packing up boxes. A woman hands us a list of the items that go in each box and sends us off to the canned-food shelves. She looks vaguely familiar to me, but I can't place her. Zack tosses me a can of yams, and as I place it in the cardboard box it suddenly hits me where I've seen her before. The supermarket—she's Billy's mother!

Hands shaking, I leave Zack as he's about to throw me a can of cranberry sauce. Weaving through the crowd, I find her piling bags of stuffing onto a table.

I take a deep breath and tap her on the shoulder. "You're Billy's mother, right?"

She turns around and scans my face. I can tell she's coming up empty. "Do I know you?" she asks, holding onto a large bag of stuffing.

"Not really," I admit. "But a few months ago my mother and I were in line at the supermarket in front of you and your son. He told me my name was purple and orange, and I tried to call you but your number—"

She holds up her hand to stop me. "I'm so sick of that 'colors' nonsense. I don't know where he gets his imagination from. He's so different from his sister. She never tried to fill people's heads with this sort of thing. She's a cheerleader. About your age, I'd guess. Her name's Amy, maybe you know her?"

I don't feel like telling her I'm not friends with any cheerleaders, so I just shake my head. "But about Billy, it's not his imagination. Other people see letters and numbers in color. I do, in fact."

Her grip tightens on the bag, but she doesn't say anything. I continue. "There's a meeting a few weekends from now that he could come to. I can get you the information."

"Thank you for your interest in Billy," she finally says, before abruptly turning away. She bends down to grab more bags of stuffing from the box under the table. With her back still to me, she says matter-of-factly, "But we're going to be away that weekend. I need to go back to work now, and I suggest you do the same."

I open my mouth to argue, but there's nothing more I can say. As I head back to the canned-goods area, I realize I never even told her which weekend it was.

"Why is your face all red?" Zack asks. He's already working on his second box.

I put my hand up to my cheek. It feels warm. It must be because I'd never spoken to an adult like that before. Not that it did any good.

"Do you know that woman?" he asks, glancing over in her direction.

"Not really." I double-check that Zack packed the box up correctly and discover he had included three bags of marshmallows and no green beans. While we work on the boxes I work on convincing myself that Billy will turn out all right without any interference from me.

About an hour later my father comes over to get us. Most families have left by now, and I'm exhausted. I'm fumbling with the buttons on my coat when Billy appears before me. He had been in the baby-sitting section all this time.

"Hi, Mia!" he says in his squeaky little-boy's voice.

"Hey, Billy boy." I bend down, and he flies into my arms. I'm a bit surprised, but I return the hug.

"It's waaaaay past my bedtime," he informs me in a whisper.

"Mine too," I whisper in return. His mother has sighted us and hurries over. She takes him by the hand and gives me a look of annoyance and suspicion.

"Bye-bye, Mia!" Billy calls as his mother yanks him out the door. I wave to him as the door closes between us. "Good luck, Billy," I whisper sadly.

When I get home I find an e-mail from Adam waiting for me.

DEAR MIA,

I DID SOME RESEARCH FOR YOU. I THINK WHAT YOU SAW WERE PEOPLE'S PHEROMONES IN ACTION. THERE MUST BE SOME SYNESTHETIC CONNECTION. BEFORE YOU ASK WHAT A PHEROMONE IS, I'LL GIVE YOU THE DEFINITION FROM THE INTERNET: "A CHEMICAL SUBSTANCE INVISIBLE TO THE EYE THAT ALL ANIMALS AND HUMANS EMIT. THESE EMISSIONS ARE INTENDED TO SOMEHOW INFLUENCE ANOTHER PERSON'S OR ANIMAL'S BEHAVIOR. ONE ANIMAL, SAY A LION, WILL EMIT A CHEMICAL INTO THE AIR TO

ATTRACT A LIONESS. THE LIONESS WILL SENSE IT AND WILL GO TO HIM. THIS IS ALL VERY UNCONSCIOUS. THEY DON'T REALIZE THEY'RE DOING IT." IT MUST HAVE BEEN A REALLY NEAT EXPERIENCE. TELL ME MORE. ADAM

My cheeks burn when I think of Roger sending his tendrils out to me. "I saw this happen with people," I whisper in awe. How can Roger want me to come to him like a lioness? He barely even talks to me or looks my way.

The next morning Roger finds me at my locker before homeroom. He doesn't say hello; he just launches in. "Would you mind going to the acupuncturist on Tuesday instead of Wednesday? Since Wednesday's the day before Thanksgiving, Faith is switching her schedule."

"That'd be great," I tell him, hoping I don't sound too eager.

The homeroom warning bell rings. "Well, I guess I should go," Roger says. "See you in history." He walks away, his limp less noticeable.

"See?" a voice says from behind me. "I told you so."

I don't need to turn around to know it's Zack. "What exactly did you tell me?"

"That he looooves you."

"You're ridiculous, Zack. And you're going to be late for homeroom."

"It's okay. My teacher looooves me."

It figures. Everyone always loves Zack.

After school, Jenna and I ride our bikes down the bumpy road to the country store to get decorations for her party. We don't bother to lock up our bikes since there's no one around to steal them. Whenever we come down here I feel like we're characters from *Little House on the Prairie*. We've known Old Mike, the owner of the store, since we were tall enough to reach the candy shelf. When he sees us he slides a small box out from under the counter.

"I got the balloons, young ladies," he says, placing the box on the counter. "I still don't understand why anyone'd want black balloons for a party."

"It's part of the theme," Jenna explains. "Black is sophisticated."

Old Mike laughs his deep belly laugh. I'm not so sure what he's laughing at.

"Sophistication comes a little slow to these parts," he says.

"Well," Jenna replies, digging into her pocket for the money her dad gave her, "I figure it's my job to help it along." She pays for the balloons and streamers, and we head straight for the candy section. Jenna carefully scrutinizes the chocolate while I decide between the Gobstoppers and Bazooka gum. I choose both.

"So you'll never believe what Rebecca did yester-day," Jenna says offhandedly.

"Let me guess. She said something nice to you?"

"Yes! Can you believe it?" Jenna finally selects a Peppermint Patty, and we head back to the counter to pay for the candy.

"What exactly did she say?"

"She told me she could French-braid my hair for the party."

"I always knew the woman was pure evil! Are you going to let her do it?"

"No! I mean, I don't think I am. Why, do you think I should?"

I shrug. "A French braid might look sophisticated."

We say good-bye to Old Mike, take our bundles, and pack them into the basket on Jenna's bike. Before we leave, Jenna says, "I just don't want her to think I like her."

"Somehow I don't think you need to worry about that."

❧

Over the weekend I work on the Ibo slave-ship painting and try to catch up on some homework. I take a break and log on to the synesthesia Web site. There's a new article titled "How I Got over My Fear of French." It's about this woman who had to learn French for her job and was having a lot of trouble. I scan the article hungrily, hoping it can help me learn Spanish. After trying many different ways of matching up her colored letters, she finally found something that worked. For her the color of *dog* in English is green, but the French word, *chien*, is light blue. So to remember how to say *dog* in French, she pictures being on a street in France and remembers that the *French* dog is light blue. I don't know if that would work for me, but it's worth a try. Someday I'll get around to it.

When Tuesday afternoon finally arrives I feel like I'm going to burst if I don't lie on that acupuncture table soon. I'm so fidgety in the car that Roger asks me if I want to go first this time. How can I say no?

Finally, the time has come. Faith asks me how my ears are feeling, and it takes me a second to remember my earache. I tell her my ears feel better, but they still hurt. She nods and explains that the mild electric currents might help speed up the healing process. Once all of the needles are in place, the balls instantly reappear. A sigh of relief escapes my lips. I don't even need to open my eyes to tell that the brownish-pink glow around her is back too. I'm magic again!

A humming noise alerts me to the fact that the electric current has been switched on. I feel a slight pulling on the needles as she attaches the wires.

Then fireworks go off in my head.

Chapter Twelve

My eyes snap open and everything is so bright that I have to close them again. The colors are everywhere, filling all space. I am overwhelmed, and for a second it scares me, like the time Zack set all my alarm clocks to go off at once. But this is different. There's no noise; all the multicolored balls, zigzags, and spirals are coming from inside me. I slowly open my eyes, and things are a little calmer now. The glow around Faith is ten times as vibrant as it was the first time, and the last vestige of guilt caused by lying to my parents leaves me. I'm sure they wouldn't deny me this experience if they knew about it.

Eventually, I become aware of Faith's voice telling me I have to get up so Roger can come in. When did she take the needles out? I quickly get to my feet and then hold on to the table while a wave of dizziness passes. I walk out into the waiting room in a daze. Everything seems alive. The brown carpet looks like a deep, plush forest floor. The fruit in the bowl on the desk is practically pulsating with life. Roger passes me on his way to the office, and the trail of red he leaves behind is so thick I feel as though I should be able to touch it. I drop the envelope with my forty dollars in it on the desk. A full two months' allowance, but oh so worth it.

I try to read while Roger has his turn, but there's no way I can concentrate on anything as two-dimensional as a magazine. Mrs. Carson keeps glancing at me, and I wonder if I'm acting strangely. I cross my legs and try to stop tapping my feet. It seems like forever until he comes out and we can go outdoors. Everything's brimming with life! The bushes, the birds, me and Roger, Roger's mother, and everyone else. Things that people have touched, such as parking meters and door handles, all have colored smears on them.

"Hey, watch out!" Roger says loudly, grabbing me by my sweater. "What's wrong with you?"

"Huh?"

"You were about to walk out into traffic."

"Oh." I look up and find myself standing about a foot into the street. I quickly back up onto the sidewalk. "Thanks."

He looks at me with concern, and we hurry to catch up with his mother.

As soon as I get into the house I'm bombarded with the colors of my family. Just by the patches in the air I can tell who has recently been in which rooms. I'm surprised I don't see more of the mango-colored smear along the floors. That changes when I get upstairs. I can clearly see the trail Mango left behind him when he went back and forth between the litter box and the foot of my bed. It looks as if he didn't travel too far today. I spring onto the bed next to him and think about how crazy all this would sound if I told anyone. They would never believe me.

I try hard to act normal at dinner, and for once I'm glad Dad's busy outside. He's the most perceptive person in the family. Apparently there's going to be a big drop in temperature in a few days, and he needs to empty the fluids in the helicopter so they don't freeze.

"I expect everyone to help for Thanksgiving," my mother says, slipping into her frantic tone. "We've only got two days left, and I haven't even picked up the turkey."

Beth puts her fork down. "Are you aware that each year forty-five million turkeys are killed for Thanksgiving? Not to mention the twenty-two million at Christmas."

Silence. Then my mother says, "I suppose we could have chicken instead." She glances down at the lightly fried chicken that everyone except Beth is eating for dinner.

"Do you have any idea how many chickens are killed in America each year?" Beth's eyes are blazing, and little balls shoot off of her head.

Mom sighs. "I bet you're going to tell us."

"Eight *billion!*" Beth cries.

"Billion?" Zack asks, putting down the drumstick he was gnawing on.

"I think it's time to start a new Thanksgiving tradition," Beth declares, pounding her fist on the table. "Tofu loaf! Who's with me?"

"I'm with you," Zack says, rising from his seat.

"Save the turkeys," I add, and stand beside him. My green cloud entwines with his silver one, and I feel the recent tension between us lift a little.

My mother sighs. "Your father isn't going to like it."

"It's possible he won't notice," Zack offers.

I leave them to work out the details. I attempt to do my homework and don't even get through my first class. My slave-ship painting is due tomorrow, and I complete it as best I can. It's really hard to focus with the green and orange smudges from Mango and me all over the room. I wipe off my brushes and stand back to contemplate the finished product. Well, it certainly isn't my best work, but it will have to do.

The next morning I can't believe it when my alarm goes off and I can still see the green glow around my arm. Mango is still glowing at the bottom of the bed. He's slightly less bright than he was last night, but only slightly. For a second I wonder if I should be worried that the effects of the acupuncture haven't worn off. Then I decide to just enjoy it since in a matter of hours I surely won't be magic anymore.

Just walking through the halls at school is a totally overwhelming experience. The hall is filled with layers of color. It's beautiful to watch, but I tend to keep bumping into people. Balls and tendrils are floating everywhere, and of course I'm late for homeroom. After homeroom we have a Thanksgiving assembly, and then the rest of our classes will be shortened. The halls are full again as everyone pours into the auditorium. I hang back from the crowd and only look up when someone calls my name.

"We were looking for you," Laura says. Roger is with her.

"You were?" I can't muster up any enthusiasm.

"We wanted to see the painting before class."

Oh no, the painting! I left it at home! "I have to go," I tell them and fight my way through the crowd without looking back. The halls empty out as I get farther away from the auditorium, and no one sees me go into the phone booth. I say a little prayer in the hope that one of my parents will be home.

"Hello?"

I've never been so happy to hear my father's voice. I tell him he needs to bring me the slave-ship painting from my room. It's all wrapped up and ready to go.

"Can't it wait till tomorrow?" he asks.

"Dad, tomorrow's Thanksgiving."

"Oh, right. Hey, shouldn't the turkey be defrosting? I'm in the kitchen, and I don't see a turkey."

"I'm sure Mom has it under control." No way I'm going to be the one to break the news to him. "Dad, you have to hurry and get here before the end of the assembly."

"All right, all right, I'll leave right now." He mutters something as he hangs up, but all I can make out is the word turkey.

I pace the hall outside the phone booth, unsure what to do with myself. There's no way I can stay in the assembly with all those people, but if I stand out here, someone's going to make me show a hall pass soon. A door swings open across from me, and two giggling girls come out from the bathroom. I wait until they turn the corner and then duck inside. I keep busy by reading the bathroom walls. "Janey loves Jeff." "I hate algebra." "For a good time call Hank." In comparison to the new colors I see around people, my colored letters now seem very dim. After I finish with the walls,

I sit on the window ledge and watch the outside world go by. When I'm bored of that, I examine myself in the mirror, and the harsh light lets me see every pore on my face. It's not a pretty sight. I notice that I can't see my green glow in the mirror. I read somewhere that vampires don't show up in mirrors. Maybe I'm turning into a vampire. At this point nothing would surprise me.

Whenever another girl comes in I start washing my hands. If I have to do it one more time, my skin will flake right off. Finally, I decide to brave the hallway and wait by the main door. Dad's truck pulls up a minute later, and he honks hello. I cringe and look behind me to make sure no one heard it. The coast is clear, so I run out and grab the painting from the backseat.

"No hug?" he says, getting out of the truck to stretch.

"My arms are full, Dad. I'll owe you one, okay? Thanks for this." I turn back and run into the school just as the hall fills with students again. Although only fifty minutes have passed, everyone's glow is much dimmer, and it's considerably easier to walk straight. I say a prayer of thanks to the god of synesthesia for both the experience and for making the experience fade away. I also throw one in to the god of Thanksgiving assemblies.

As soon as the first group is done talking about the McCarthy hearings, it's our turn. We meet at the front of the room, and I lean the painting up on the chalkboard. At least I won't have to speak. Laura, Roger, and Jonah take turns reciting the story of the Ibos and their plight. Mrs. Morris seems captivated, and the class actually pays attention. When we're done, Mrs. Morris asks us to talk about the painting. The other three turn to me expectantly. I haven't stood up and spoken in front of a class since that fateful day in third grade. I freeze and look pleadingly at Roger. He silently gestures for me to go ahead. I pause for a second and see that all three of them are sending out faded tendrils and balls in my direction. They're trying to give me support. I take a shallow breath and look at the painting, instead of at the class, while I talk.

"Um, well, I painted the slave ship lost at sea to show that the souls of some of the Ibo are still not at rest." I glance at Roger, who motions with his hand for me to say more. "And, uh, I used watercolor paint because it can wash away easily, just like the memory of the Ibo revolt unless we keep studying it." I step away from the painting to show I'm done speaking. The class claps for us, and Mrs. Morris says she wants to hang the painting in the classroom. She pulls on the rubber gloves she keeps in her top drawer and lifts the painting by the corners.

"It's not wet anymore," I tell her, moving out of her way.

"Yes, well, just in case," she replies. I realize she's protecting her hands from germs, not wet paint. It's hard not to be a little insulted.

"Where did you run off to this morning?" Roger hisses at me as we make our way to our seats. His tendrils are active, but not in my direction. I'd have thought he would have complimented me on my explanation of the picture, but no.

"I already know all about the Pilgrims and the Indians," I hiss in return.

"Very funny," he says. "You left it at home, didn't you?"

By the time I recover myself enough to reply, he's in his seat and looking away.

It's weird that Thanksgiving always comes on a Thursday. Yesterday I was in school, and today it's this big family-holiday thing. It's kind of jarring. In my opinion, we should get the whole week off, like for Christmas. By the time we sit down for Thanksgiving dinner, the glows around everyone have faded even more. Now they're just a soft glimmer. For some reason, Mango's color is the brightest. Dad didn't speak to Mom all morning because of the turkey-tofu switcheroo. He finally caved in around three this afternoon when Beth convinced him that Thanksgiving is about giving thanks for the freedom of all living things, and that includes the turkeys.

Today is the second Thanksgiving since Grandpa died, and it just isn't the same without him. It was his favorite holiday. He used to take some of the cornstalks that Jenna's father gave us and make tie-dyed patterns on the corn with food coloring. After a while the corn would start to stink, but it made the table look very festive. It's too quiet without him here. Mango is curled up in a ball under my chair, and I silently thank him for bringing some piece of Grandpa back to the table, even if I'm the only one who knows it. The vet told us to keep Mango inside during the cold weather, so he hasn't been allowed out in a while. He finally stopped pacing by the back door and now just stares longingly out the windows. I reach down and give him a morsel of tofu loaf. He wrinkles his nose at it.

After dinner Mom takes a well-deserved break in the living room while the rest of us clean up. We were planning on going up to the cemetery, but it's freezing outside and Mom won't let us go. The cold front has definitely arrived. We make a lot of noise in the kitchen, maybe to make up for the quiet dinner. Raising his voice above the banging pots, Dad asks me if I'm excited about the synesthesia meeting.

I nod. But I don't know if I'm more nervous or more excited about meeting everyone—especially Adam. I'm glad there's a short session on Friday night so by Saturday I'll feel more comfortable with everyone. I hope. And with Jenna's birthday party on Saturday night, this is going to be a big weekend.

"So what time does the freak show start?" Zack asks as he plops his dirty plate into the soapy-water-filled sink.

"Zack!" my father says, flicking his dishcloth at him. "Apologize to your sister."

"I'm sorry, Mia," Zack says, lowering his eyes demurely.

"No, you're not," I reply.

"I'm a little sorry?"

"You're just upset because Beth has to baby-sit for you while we're gone."

"I don't need a baby-sitter," Zack exclaims in a horrified tone. "I'm elev—"

"I think what Mia's doing is groovy," Beth interrupts.

The three of us turn to stare at her, and Dad lets his dish towel fall to the ground.

"Groovy?" Zack repeats.

"What is it?" she asks innocently. "I'm not allowed to say something nice to Mia in the spirit of Thanksgiving?"

"Why don't we all try to make the spirit of Thanksgiving last year round?" my father suggests, retrieving his towel and shaking it out. "Wouldn't that be nice?"

"Sure, Dad," Zack says. "No problem."

For the rest of the night we try to be nice to each other. This requires that the three of us stay at opposite ends of the house. Zack is on the computer, Beth is showing Mom some new yoga moves, and I'm throwing every item of clothing I have onto the floor in search of the perfect outfit for tomorrow night. I finally wind up sneaking into Beth's room and taking her blue-and-white-striped dress from the back of her closet. She outgrew it two years ago but has always refused to let me have it. Throwing off my clothes, I slip the dress over my head and look at myself in her full-length mirror. The sleeves are a little long, but other than that it fits fine. A little twirl makes the skirt flare up. The dress makes me feel something I usually don't—*girly*. Laughter from downstairs reminds me I only have a small window of time to act if I want permission to wear the dress. I quickly change back into my own clothes and bring the dress downstairs with me. Beth is still in the living room in a pose she calls a "downward-facing dog." I ask sweetly if I can borrow the dress, and she has no choice but to say yes since Mom is in the room and it's Thanksgiving and all. I can feel her glaring at my back as I go up the stairs, but I don't care. I'm feeling girly, and I'm going to meet a boy tomorrow night.

Chapter Thirteen

The rhythm of the rain on the windshield of Dad's truck would almost be soothing if I weren't so crazed with anticipation. I'm trying not to fidget because every time I shift in my seat the torn vinyl scratches the backs of my legs. Dad's truck might handle better in the rain than Mom's car, but no one would call it comfortable. The ride to the university seems endless, and it's so dark out that I can't even watch the scenery.

"Are we almost there yet?" I ask for the tenth time. Neither of my parents bothers to answer me. In fact, they haven't answered me the last eight times. It's not my fault it's too dark and rainy to figure out where we are. Maybe I should have worn pants. Jerry said that most synesthetes are female, but the only ones I know about—Billy and Adam—are boys. What if I'm the only girl at the meeting? I'm sure I'm the youngest. What if I say something stupid? Maybe I shouldn't say anything at all.

Finally my mother points out a sign on the side of

the road that says UNIVERSITY HOUSE, 2 MILES. Jerry rented the building from the school for the weekend and said it has a cozy atmosphere. As we pull up alongside the house, I can see smoke billowing out of the chimney. I step out of the car, push open my umbrella, and shiver.

The door opens as we approach it, and Debbie pops her head out. She beams at me and waves us in. I can hear voices talking and laughing in the next room.

"You must be Mr. Winchell," Debbie says, pumping my dad's hand. She then turns to my mother. "We're so glad you both could come. Everyone else is here already, Mia. Ready to meet them?"

My legs don't seem to want to move. I nod mutely.

"Here, let me take your coat first."

I slip off my coat and pass it to Debbie along with my dripping umbrella. She squeezes them into a small closet and leans her weight against the door to close it. Then she links her arm in mine and leads me toward the other room. My parents follow a few steps behind.

"Here we are," she announces. I stare into what looks like a normal living room with couches, chairs, and a fireplace. About fifteen unfamiliar faces turn toward us. The talking gradually stops as they wait for Debbie to introduce me. I'd say three quarters of the group are women, of which I'm by far the youngest. I see Adam right away, since he's the only other teen-ager in the room. He looks a little like Roger, except his face is rounder and he has darker hair. He also has a big smile that covers practically the whole bottom half of his face. I guess he knows who I am too. I scan the other faces but don't see Jerry anywhere. I'm relieved to see that the glows around everyone are so faint that they won't distract me.

"This is Mia Winchell," Debbie says, pushing me in front of her. "She's been working with us here in Chicago."

"Hi, Mia," everyone says.

"Hi," I answer in a small voice. I quickly see I'm dressed appropriately and relax a little. My parents slip over to the folding chairs in the corner.

Jerry enters from the other end of the room with a tray of food, and his face lights up when he sees me.

"Mia! Grab a spot on the couch. Helen will move over, won't you, Helen?"

Helen is about sixty years old and is wearing the most colorful patchwork dress I've ever seen.

"Sure I will," Helen says, scooping up her skirt and patting the space beside her. I walk into the room and sit, amazed I didn't trip over the people sitting on the floor. Helen pats me on the knee, and her long ear-rings swish back and forth.

"Now that we're all here," Jerry says, settling into a chair by the fire, "let's go around one last time and introduce ourselves."

The group groans good-naturedly. Jerry adds, "This time please go into more detail about your own synesthesia."

The introductions begin, and if the kids at school think *I'm* strange, they wouldn't *believe* some of these people. One woman sees colors and shapes whenever she eats cold food. Another woman swears that her numbers not only have color, but also have personalities. Three other people in the room jump up and swear *their* numbers have personalities too. A lively debate arises over whether the number eight is shy or a flirt. I listen in awe, stealing glances at Adam whenever possible.

"Eight is definitely a flirt," one of the women declares. "Because three is shy, four is rude, and two is, like, your buddy. I hated taking math in school because I always felt bad making numbers who didn't like each other work together."

"I felt the same way," a guy in his twenties adds. "Try explaining to your math teacher that you feel guilty pairing a six with a two!"

I can see my parents' raised eyebrows from across the room. I'm glad they won't be here for the next two days. I give a quick shake of my head to indicate that they don't have to worry—my numbers do not have personalities. Not that it wouldn't make things interesting, but I have enough problems with math without adding guilt to the mix.

When Adam's turn comes he speaks clearly and makes eye contact with everyone around the circle. I'm impressed. He must have a lot of confidence.

I'm so engrossed in what people are saying that I don't realize it's almost my turn to speak until Helen stands up next to me. She clears her throat and then recites a poem from Shakespeare. At least I'm assuming it's from Shakespeare, since we don't start reading him until ninth grade. After the poem she wipes a small tear from the corner of her eye and says, "I've been reading poetry since I was a young girl. I choose the poems with the prettiest-colored words. Then it's like a beautiful garden of colors appears before my very eyes."

My turn has arrived. I babble for a few minutes about my colors, wishing I could tell them about seeing the pheromones. But I don't dare tell them with my parents in the room. People are nodding as I speak, and it's so cool to be in a whole roomful of people who understand me. Adam gives me a thumbs-up when I'm done.

The last person to speak is a man who looks about my father's age but is much heavier. He explains that color rules his life. He picks his friends based on whether he likes or dislikes the colors of their names. He even chooses his food that way. "Unfortunately," he says, pointing to his large belly, "my favorite color is the pale green of the word *chocolate!*" He adds that he has to turn off his car radio in order to concentrate in traffic. Half of the room nods in agreement. I'll have to remember that when I take my driving test in three years.

People start yelling things out now. The oldest man in the room — he looks like he's around seventy — says he married his first wife because her name tasted like peanut butter. Then he met this other woman whose name tasted like peaches, his favorite food, so he divorced the first one and married the second! One woman brags that she can read and write upside down and backward, and that when she writes with her right hand, her left hand can follow along and write the same sentence backward. Three other women call out that they do that too. I hadn't thought about it in years, but I used to do that when I was little. It never crossed my mind that it might be connected to my colors. I guess whatever "wires" are mixed up in my brain are responsible for all sorts of strange things.

Jerry waits until the room quiets down and asks, "Does anyone want to share their word-pictures? Let's raise our hands this time."

Three hands shoot up, but then they all start talking at once. I guess I'm about to find out what a word-picture is.

"The name *Jerry* is like a big sugar cube with chopsticks sticking out of it…"

"No, it's not, it's like a bicycle pump with a red handle…"

"No way, it's a big pillow with the stuffing being squeezed out."

The rest of us look at one another and shrug. I imagine their heads must get pretty crowded if every word has a picture with it. Since we have an early day tomorrow, Jerry tells us to mingle for a little while and then call it a night. The rest of the weekend will be taken up with experiments. I feel like I'm part of an elite club and can't wait for tomorrow. It hardly seems possible that I had once wanted my synesthesia to go away. Adam motions me over to the fireplace, where he holds out his hand.

"We haven't been formally introduced," he says in a pretend grown-up voice.

I reach out to shake his hand. He grabs it and kisses the back of it. He actually kisses my hand! Fortunately my parents have wandered out of the room or else I'd be mortified.

"Charmed, Miss Winchell," he says, lightly dropping my hand. "Adam Dickson at your service." He tugs at the collar of his thick sweater. "It's a little hot in here, isn't it? The rain has stopped; maybe we should go outside for some air?" It *has* gotten a little stuffy in the room. Of course it could be because we're standing in front of the fire. Before I can say anything, Adam takes my hand and leads me out a back door and into a little courtyard. I'm so energized that I barely feel the cold. We sit down on a bench that had been partially sheltered from the rain. I've never been in the dark with a boy before. Well, other than Zack of course. My palms are sweating, and I wipe them on my dress.

"So this is pretty great, right?" Adam says. I'm not sure if he means the meeting or us sitting on the bench together.

"Uh-huh," I say, figuring it's a safe answer.

"Where did this come from?" he asks, lightly touching my friendship bracelet. His fingers graze my arm, and I shiver a little as I tell him about the bracelet.

"Are you cold?" he asks, moving a little closer. "We should have grabbed a bottle of wine from inside; they never would have noticed. That would warm you right up."

"Really, I'm fine," I tell him. "Didn't you get really sick the last time you drank?"

"Oh, that. I was just a kid then."

Before I can ask what he thinks he is now, he says, "You look just like I thought you would. Am I like you pictured?"

"I don't know, I didn't really—"

"Mia?" he interrupts.

"Yes?"

"Can I kiss you?"

"What?" I ask a little too loudly.

"Never mind," he says, looking across the yard.

"No, I mean, it's okay. I mean, yes, you can." I stop rambling and he smiles at me. If my palms weren't already sweating, they would be right now. It was about time I had my first kiss. It seems fitting that it should be with another synesthete, since we understand each other so well.

I close my eyes and feel his lips touch mine. Our noses bump and I giggle.

"That wasn't so bad, was it?" he asks, smiling.

I shake my head, afraid to say anything stupid. He leans in to kiss me again.

Suddenly I hear footsteps behind us. "Mia!"

I cringe and pull away from Adam. My mother

doesn't look happy to see me kissing a strange boy on a bench in the dark.

I hurry to introduce Adam, explaining that we knew each other already.

"That's great," she snaps, and practically drags me away by my sleeve. All I can do is wave good-bye.

"See you tomorrow, Mia," he calls out after us. "Nice meeting you, Mrs. Winchell."

My mother grunts in reply and hands me my coat. I wonder if she's this hard on Beth's boyfriends. Not that Adam is my boyfriend or anything. I don't even know if I want him to be.

I think about whether or not I'd want him as a boyfriend the whole ride home. I'm still thinking about it as I pick through the Thanksgiving leftovers. Not surprisingly, there's a lot of the tofu loaf left. It actually tastes better the day after. Maybe it tastes better because everything tastes better when you are wearing old flannel pajamas at midnight.

It suddenly dawns on me that I have to get up again in six hours in order to get to the university by nine o'clock. I quickly rewrap what's left of the tofu loaf and toss my fork into the sink. On the way out of the kitchen I pass Mango's food dish and see that it's still mostly full from this morning. I bet he's still stuffed from all the Thanksgiving table scraps Zack fed him when our parents weren't looking. There's a thin orange glow in front of the food dish, the last trace of my "magic" powers. I think it's very interesting that everyone else's glow is almost completely gone, but I can still see Mango's.

My thick socks are perfect for skating in the smooth hallway, and I have to grab onto the staircase to avoid crashing into the front door. As I come to a stop the full moon shining through the living-room window beckons to me. Even though it's freezing outside, I feel like sitting out on the front porch.

Grabbing my coat from the front closet, I quietly open the front door and slip outside. The top step seems dry enough, so I sit down and watch the clouds pass quickly in front of the moon. It seems impossible to believe I was just in a room with fourteen other people just like me. I can't wait to tell them about the acupuncture, which, as cool as it was, did get to be pretty distracting. But if my abilities had been stronger tonight, I would have been able to see exactly what Adam was feeling when he kissed me. That could have been useful.

A light drizzle turns the air to mist, and by the time I get back up to my room, a steady rain is pounding the ground. I climb under the warm comforter without even bothering to brush my teeth.

Sometime around three-thirty in the morning, a loud burst of thunder wakes me. I raise my head to look for Mango, who hates the thunder. Even in the darkness I can see the orange glow. I reach down to bring him into my arms, but my hands land on an empty blanket. As if on cue, a flash of lightning shows me that Mango is definitely not on the bed. The only thing there is, is a Mango-shaped space. I sit up and try to remember when I saw him last. I must have given him his medicine before I went to bed. But why can't I remember giving it to him? My memory used to be so good, but last night is all a blur. I stare at the Winnie-the-Pooh blanket, mentally willing Mango to appear.

It doesn't work.

As I'm concentrating I notice a faint orange trail leading off the bed and out my door. I decide to follow it. When I get to the front hall I have to choose between the thick orange trail leading down to the kitchen and the very faint trail leading straight to the front door. My heart pounding, I open the front door to find Mango curled up in a tight little ball on the doormat. He looks so cold. I quickly gather him in my arms, and he sluggishly opens one eye, then lets it close again. Holding him tight against my chest, I push the door closed with my hip and hurry back to bed. We lie there, under the comforter, as my body heat slowly warms him. I spend the next hour holding and nuzzling him, alternately wondering how I didn't see him slip outside, hating myself for letting him get so cold, and debating whether or not I should give him another pill. Mango might not know any better than to go outside in the freezing cold, but the part of him that's Grandpa should've. Maybe the Grandpa part was asleep at the time. Finally Mango starts purring, and I let my eyes close.

The next time I wake up it's a few hours later, and the clacking of the furnace almost drowns out the sound of Mango's heavy wheezing. Almost. I try to wake him up, but he won't respond. Then he starts twitching his arms and legs but still won't wake up. For the second time that night I jump out of bed and run into the hall. This time I run to my parents' room and knock frantically on their door. My mother opens it and immediately looks worried.

"What is it, Mia?"

I'm wringing my hands, and my heart feels like it's going to burst in my chest. "We have to take Mango to the vet right away. There's something wrong with him! Please hurry!"

Together we run back to my room. She takes one look at Mango, who is still twitching, and tells me to wrap him in a blanket and meet her in the car. I slip on my rain boots and briefly wonder whether I should put real clothes on. Another twitch from Mango makes the decision for me. I grab the Pooh blanket, wrap him up in it, and head downstairs. My mother, also in her pajamas and rain boots, is hanging up the phone in the kitchen.

"What did the vet say?" I ask, terrified of the answer.

"The storm last night flooded the main road," my mother says helplessly. "She can't get to her office, and we can't get to her house."

I stare at my mother as I digest this information. "We'll have to take the helicopter," I say, panic building in my chest. "It's not raining anymore, right?"

Mango wheezes loudly, and my mother tells me to wait by the door while she runs back upstairs. I wait by the stairs, my ears buzzing with fear as every second seems like an hour. Finally my father appears, hopping on one foot as he pulls on his thick boots.

"Where will we land, Dad?" I ask, my throat tight.

"Leave it to me," he says. "Wait here while I warm up the engine."

I watch him run across the rain-soaked field and disappear into the cockpit. I remember how Mango's mango-colored wheezes used to be comforting because they meant he was still around. They are anything *but* comforting now. Mom and Zack join me in the kitchen. Zack gently strokes Mango's head while we wait. Every few seconds I feel a twitch through the thin blanket, and my stomach flip-flops.

Dad flashes the lights on and off, signaling he's ready for me. I race outside, hunched over to keep Mango warm. I climb in and strap myself into the seat. Still holding Mango tight, I lower my head and rest it on his as the propeller speeds up. The helicopter begins to lift and then settles right back down again, the propeller sputtering. I realize I'm holding my breath, and I force myself to breathe. Tears slip out as I exhale.

"Hurry, Dad, please!" I'm pleading and crying at the same time.

"I'm trying, Mia, just hold on." He makes some adjustments on the panel, and the propeller slowly winds up again.

"Hold on, Mango," I beg as I gently pet him. "You'll be better soon, I promise."

Mango meows softly. I feel a second of relief, thinking maybe he understood me and knows we're trying to get help. The helicopter starts to lift again, and it takes my brain a second to realize that something is different. Mango isn't twitching anymore. He isn't wheezing. He isn't breathing.

"Dad! Stop!" The chopper bumps back down.

My fingers shake uncontrollably as I unwrap the blanket and stare down at Mango. He looks like he's asleep except his chest isn't moving. I shake him but nothing happens.

"Turn him onto his back," my father commands.

Time has stopped. The only things that exist in the world are me, my father, and Mango. The tears are streaming down my face now and making Mango's fur wet. My father tips Mango's head back and breathes into his mouth and nose. Then he presses lightly against Mango's chest with two fingers. My head is swimming, and I feel like I'm going to pass out. After a minute of this Dad looks up at me, his face ashen, and shakes his head.

My eyes open wide, and the pain hits me in thick black waves. Then I scream loud enough to wake the dead.

Only it doesn't.

Chapter Fourteen

I refuse to get out of this seat. The rest of the family is in the helicopter now, and Mango is on the floor in front of Beth, rewrapped in his blanket. I can't even look at him. I am dimly aware that Zack and Beth are crying and that my parents are whispering. I still have my seat belt on and am hunched over my knees, gagging. It feels like someone kicked me in the stomach, only a hundred times worse. This can't be happening, this isn't real, this is not my life. If I keep repeating this, maybe I'll wake up from this nightmare. I was so happy last night. Now I can't feel my legs. My chest is burning, and the numbness in my head blocks out everything else.

"Mia?" my father says in a low, gentle voice as he touches my shoulder. "Why don't we all go in the house now?"

Still hunched over, I shake my head vehemently.

"C'mon, Mia," my mother says. "It's no use sitting out here. I think it's starting to hail."

The sound of ice pelting the chopper breaks through

the haze in my head. From some dark corner of my brain I realize I can't see the colored shapes that would normally accompany the sound. All I see are gray blobs that look like used chewing gum. In fact, when the helicopter was moving, the propeller noise didn't have any color either. The last color I remember seeing is the orange from Mango's wheezes when I held him. I've lost everything.

My mother has unbuckled my seat belt, and she helps me up before I can protest further. My eyes fall on Mango's stiff shape on the floor, and a fresh torrent of tears flows from my eyes. Mom grabs my arms to keep me from falling back into my seat.

I follow my mother and Zack out of the chopper, vaguely aware that Dad and Beth have stayed behind. In a daze, I walk slowly back to the house, barely noticing that I'm being struck by tiny chunks of ice. My coat and the front of my pajamas are instantly wet. I wish the ice would go right through me and take all the pain away.

I go straight to my room, not caring that I'm tracking water and mud through the house. Locking the door behind me, I strip off my wet pajamas and throw on a fresh pair. I want to smash things. I want to grab my precious clocks off the wall and hurl them across the room. So I do the only logical thing — I climb back into bed and pull the covers over my head. *It's just a dream*, I tell myself, curling into a tight ball. I'll wake up for real, and everything will be back to normal. My eyes shut tight; I force myself to take a deep breath. Opening my eyes, I peek out from under the covers and look down at the end of the bed. All I see is a colorless Mango-shaped space and Mango's beloved Tweety Bird. I grab the small stuffed animal and hold it against my chest. There are little holes all over it from where Mango carried it with his pointy cat teeth. I start to shake, and the tears come so quickly that my eyes burn. Why did Mango have to go out in the cold? He knew he wasn't supposed to. How is it possible that I'll never hold him or pet him or hear his wheezes again? He's gone, and he took what was left of Grandpa's soul with him. I'm all alone. Did Mango know how much I loved him?

A while later a knock on the door prompts me to bolt upright, confused. I must have cried myself to sleep. Everything that happened comes crashing back in on me, and I flop back down.

"Your door's locked, Mia," my mother says, jiggling the knob.

"I know," I answer, my voice muffled by the pillow.

"I called Jerry earlier and explained why you didn't go to the meeting today," she says through the door.

"And now Adam's on the phone for you. Do you want to take it?"

It takes me a minute to piece together what she said. The meeting hadn't even entered my mind. Neither had Adam. And I didn't want to think of him now.

"I don't want to talk to him," I tell her. "Or anyone else."

"You should at least eat something. It's late afternoon already."

"I'm not hungry," I call out. I can't imagine ever being hungry again.

I wait to hear her footsteps go down the hall before I get up to go to the bathroom. The smell from the litter box wafts out of the hall closet and seems to taunt me. It says, "If you had cleaned me more, maybe Mango would have stayed around." I kick the closet door shut and hurry into the bathroom. By mistake I catch my reflection in the mirror. My eyes are red and swollen like I've been crying for a week instead of just one day. I pick up my toothbrush and almost throw it down again as the memory of my decision not to brush my teeth last night comes flooding back to me. I always used to give Mango his pill right after I washed my face and brushed my teeth. I'd have realized he was missing earlier.

Someone knocks on the door. "Come to Beth's room when you're done in there," Zack says.

I ignore him, and he knocks again.

"Go away." I place the toothbrush back in its holder, unable to use it.

"Just come when you're done."

"Not unless Beth can use her magic to bring Mango back."

Zack doesn't answer, but I can hear him out there breathing. "I...I don't think she can do that." A minute later I hear him shuffle down the hall in his feety pajamas. I guess he didn't bother to get dressed today either.

I can't face going back to my empty room yet, so a few minutes later I find myself in Beth's doorway. She and Zack are sitting in the middle of the floor inside a lopsided circle made from rope. Candles are burning on every flat surface.

"We waited for you," Beth says.

"For what?"

"It's a healing circle," Zack explains. "Beth said it will make us feel better after what happened. With Mango, I mean. We know what you're going through."

I feel the anger rise in me. "You have no idea at all what I'm going through!"

"We loved Mango too, Mia," Beth says. Zack nods vigorously.

"Not the way I loved him. And you didn't kill him.

I did. I killed Mango." As soon as the words are out of my mouth, I realize they are true. It isn't Mango that I should be mad at for leaving, it's myself, for letting him go. Like in that book we had to read in school last year, *The Little Prince*. You are responsible for what you tame. I tamed Mango. I was *responsible* for him and I failed him. I let him slip outside. I didn't give him his medication last night. I didn't pay enough attention to him lately. I put my hand over my mouth. "Oh my god," I whisper. "I killed Mango."

I can hear them calling out to me as I run down the hall to my room, but I don't stop. No brown rings appear when I slam my door. I throw myself down into my desk chair and lower my head to the smooth surface of the desk. The guilt is more than I can bear. I let Mango die. Wherever his soul is now, he must hate me. Grandpa must hate me. I lift my head too fast and get dizzy. After a minute of rifling through my bottom drawer, I find what I'm looking for. A little white box with a green piece of the moon in it. I don't deserve to have this special gift from Grandpa anymore. Shoving open my window, I open the box and let its contents fall onto the front lawn. I toss the empty box into the wastebasket and slam the window shut. I don't feel any better.

The phone rings with no red spirals. A minute later my mother comes to tell me it's Jenna.

"Tonight's her birthday party, right?" my mother asks as I follow her, zombielike, back to her bedroom. "Mia," she says in a gentle voice, "why don't you think about going?"

I stare at her incredulously. "Did you tell her what happened today?"

"No, I thought you would want to."

I brace myself and reluctantly pick up the phone. "Jenna?"

She launches right into the attack. "Why aren't you here yet? I have something important that I wanted to give you before the party started. Molly and Kimberly have been here for over an hour helping me set up."

"I'm sorry, I—"

"You stayed late at your big meeting this afternoon, right? Because those people are more important than me. I bet you didn't even wear our friendship bracelet to the meeting."

I flash back to Adam asking me about the bracelet and touching my arm. Was that just last night? It feels like a year ago. And that girl on the bench couldn't possibly have been me.

Jenna assumes my silence is a confirmation. "I knew it! Don't even bother to come," she says coldly and hangs up the phone.

I stand there, numbly staring at the dead receiver in my hand.

"Why didn't you tell her what happened?" my mother asks, guiding my hand to replace the phone in its cradle.

"She didn't give me a chance." I shrug. "It doesn't really matter anyway. Nobody could make me feel any worse than I already do."

"Why don't you call her back and explain?"

I shake my head. "I couldn't possibly go to the party anyway."

My mother strokes my hair, something I can't remember her doing since I was a little girl. "I think you should try to eat something now."

"I don't want to."

"Please try, that's all I ask."

I decide it's not worth arguing, and I let her take me down into the kitchen. I stare out the window at the bleak gray sky while she busily prepares me something to eat. The newspaper is on the table, and I glance at the large headline type. All the letters are black. I can sense a kind of depth to them, but their colors are gone. I almost laugh remembering how I used to wish all the letters would just be black. So now I'm no longer the girl who sees colors, and I'm no longer the girl whose grandfather's soul is in her cat. All I am is the girl who is no longer special in any way. I'm the girl who is empty. Like a deflated helium balloon. I can't believe this is how everyone else feels all the time.

Mom places a plate of wheat crackers covered with cheddar cheese on the table in front of me. I take a bite and nearly spit it out.

"What's wrong?" Mom asks.

"It tastes like wet cardboard."

"Just try to get it down."

I *was* trying to get it down, but swallowing is proving difficult. My throat is too tight. I spit the cheese and cracker out in the sink. As I stand there holding onto the counter, it dawns on me that I didn't have to step over Mango's bowls to get there. I look down. Sure enough, they're gone. I can feel the now familiar hysteria rising up in me, and I point at the ground.

"You got rid of his bowls already?" I accuse my mother with a shaky voice. "How could you do that?"

Jumping to her feet, my mother says, "Your father thought it would be best if—"

"And where's Mango?" I'm screaming now. "Did Dad throw Mango away too?"

"Mango's out in the woodshed, Mia. Just calm down."

I honestly feel like my heart is shattering into a million pieces at the thought of Mango lying alone in the cold shed. In an instant I'm out the back door and running to the tiny shack. Mom calls out that I'm not wearing shoes, but I ignore her and swing open the flimsy wooden door. There he is in the corner, still wrapped in his Pooh blanket. I take a step toward him and then can't make myself get closer. I kneel on the cold, hard floor and cover my face with my hands.

"I'm so sorry, Mango," I whisper over and over as the tears warm my cheeks and hands. "I loved you so much. You were the best cat. It's all my fault."

My mother appears at my side and puts her hand firmly on my shoulder. "Mango loved you very much, Mia. You gave him a wonderful life."

"I killed him," I state matter-of-factly, not looking up.

"Is that what you think? That's crazy."

"We all know I'm crazy, right? Well, you don't have to worry about that anymore, because my colors are gone."

Mom hooks her hand under my elbow and lifts me upright. She puts her hands on my shoulders and looks me in the eye. I try to turn away, but she holds on.

"Look, Mia. The only thing that's crazy is the idea that you had anything to do with Mango's death. And remember, Jerry said that your colors could disappear in times of trauma. This certainly qualifies as traumatic. I'm sure they'll come back."

I wrestle free from her hold. "I don't want them to come back. I don't deserve to have them anymore. You don't understand; I *did* kill him!" I run back inside and straight to my room, which is starting to feel like a prison cell. Sometime later that night my father delivers a bowl of warm creamed-corn soup and says he's not leaving until I finish it. I shake my head repeatedly, but he stands firm and gives me the spoon. I finally choke down the soup without even tasting it and hand him back an empty bowl.

"I thought we'd have a memorial service for Mango tomorrow," Dad says, still standing by my bed. "It might help you feel better."

"I won't go."

"Maybe you'll change your mind in the morning," he says, switching off my light. I know I won't change my mind. There's no way I'm going to watch Mango being lowered into the ground. I try to sleep, and somewhere in the back of my mind I think, *Wait, I have to give Mango his pill before I fall asleep.* Sure, now I remember. When it's too late.

The next morning I awake to Zack shaking me. "We're going to start the service soon," he says. "You have to get up."

The pain comes back instantly. I cover my head with the comforter. "I told Dad I'm not going."

"What? I can't hear you."

"I'm not going," I repeat louder.

"Do you think that's what Mango would have wanted?" he asks as he storms out.

"Mango would have wanted to live," I whisper. After a few minutes I make myself get out of bed and brush my teeth. The bathroom window looks out onto the backyard, where Dad is hacking away at the nearly frozen ground with a shovel. I move closer to the window and see a small wooden crate lying a few feet away from him. My stomach knots up as I realize Mango's inside it. The rest of the family stands nearby, bundled up against the cold. It must be windy too, because Beth's hair keeps whipping around her face. Suddenly she turns her head and looks right at me. She gestures for me to come down. I shake my head and back a few steps away from the window. I stand there for a minute, my arms crossed in front of me. Then I hurry back to my room, search under the covers for Tweety, and run outside in my slippers. Everyone is standing around the hole now, with the wooden crate in the center. They're holding hands and offering Mango to heaven, but I just can't do that yet. I won't.

Crying, I thrust Tweety at my father, and he lets go of Beth's hand to take it. "You'll put it in there with him?"

He nods and bends down to open the crate. I turn away before I see anything and run back into the house. I can't stay in my room anymore. I need to be far away from here. I wish I were old enough to drive. I put on my sneakers and a heavy sweater and run right past everybody into the wet fields. My mother calls out after me, but I don't turn around. I run past the ravine, which now has water coursing through it. I'm amazed that I don't fall on my face since the grass and the fallen leaves are so slippery. I keep running until I feel a sharp pain in my side. I guess the hunger is finally catching up with me. I'm only a few yards away from the cemetery, so I keep going until I reach Grandpa's headstone. I lean against it to catch my breath. It occurs to me that I never really mourned him, because I thought he was still with me. Now that I know he's really gone, it feels different being up here — sadder and definitely more final. Usually when I came here Mango was with me. I remember when I brought Grandpa his painting and Mango walked all over it. He had so much energy then, and that was only a few months ago. I hang my head and close my eyes and just try to breathe.

"Your mother thought we might find you here."

I whirl around to see Jenna, Molly, and Kimberly standing a few headstones away. They still have makeup on from the night before, and I can tell that Molly and Kimberly feel uncomfortable standing around the graves. They keep checking the ground as though they're worried that a hand will suddenly shoot up.

"What are you doing here?" I ask.

Jenna walks over and gives me a big hug before answering. I see her hair is still in a French braid from the party. "Molly and Kimberly slept over last night. Your mother called my house this morning and told us what happened."

"Yeah, Mia. I'm really sorry about Marshmallow," Kimberly says gently.

"Marshmallow?" I look at her quizzically.

"She means Mango," Jenna says, glaring at Kimberly.

Kimberly looks puzzled. "Are you sure? I thought his name was Marshmallow."

"His name was *Mango*," Molly says firmly. "I'm really sorry too, Mia. I know how much you loved him."

All I can do is nod, afraid that if I answer I'll start

crying again and won't be able to stop. I'm surprised my tear ducts still function at all.

"I'm the sorriest of all," Jenna says, her eyes filling with tears. "I was horrible on the phone last night, and I understand if you hate me."

"I don't hate you," I tell her. "You didn't know what happened."

"I didn't even give you a chance to tell me," she says, kicking the ground hard. "I don't know what's wrong with me. Maybe I was just nervous about the party."

"How did it go?" I ask. "I see you agreed to let Rebecca do your hair."

"Rebecca didn't do it; Molly did. Good old Rebecca has moved on."

I allow myself my first smile in two days. "You mean she dumped your dad?"

Jenna shakes her head. "Nope. He dumped her. At least that's what he said."

"The party wasn't the same without you," Molly assures me. "All the guys asked for you."

"*All* the guys?" I ask doubtfully.

"Well, okay, one guy. What was his name, Kimberly?"

"Roger from your history class," Kimberly answers, nervously jumping out of the way of some leaves that the wind rustled up. "I think he likes you."

"Why would you say that?" I ask, feeling my cheeks grow hot.

"Just the way he says your name. It's like *Mee-ia*," Kimberly imitates in a singsong voice.

The others laugh, and I say firmly, "He doesn't say my name that way."

Kimberly shivers. "Can we all go back to Jenna's house? No offense, but this place is a little creepy."

They have distracted me for too long. "I have to go," I tell them, practically tripping over my feet as I turn away. I start walking quickly back in the direction of the woods.

"Wait, Mia." Jenna catches up with me. "Look, I know how you feel. It's okay to be really sad."

I walk even faster. "You don't know how I feel."

She grabs onto my sweater. "How can you say that to me?"

I look her right in the eye. "You didn't kill your mother, Jenna." I leave her staring after me as I run into the woods. After a few minutes my luck runs out, and my legs suddenly shoot out in front of me. I fall flat on my butt, hard. But I barely feel the wet grass underneath me. I'm too empty.

Chapter Fifteen

That night my mother announces we're having a family meeting. "This is not optional," she says, marching us all into the kitchen. Just the smell of food makes me nauseated.

"It has come to our attention," my mother begins, "that some serious misconceptions are floating around this house."

"Somebody better catch them because I might be allergic," Zack declares. Beth kicks him under the table.

Dad picks up where Mom left off. "I know many of us are blaming ourselves for what happened, and we need to talk this out because it's very hurtful. We're all grieving in our own way, and nobody has the right to tell anyone else what to feel. But some facts can't be ignored." Turning to me, he says, "Nobody killed Mango, Mia. You knew he was sick since the day you found him. It's a blessing that we had him around as long as we did."

"It didn't feel very long," Beth says softly. For the first time I notice that her face is swollen too.

"Dad," I say, my voice shaking, "you're wrong. I didn't find Mango, Mango found me. And he expected me to take care of him, and I blew it. I left him outside in the cold Friday night. It was all my fault."

Zack stands up from the table. "No. I went outside while you guys were at the meeting. It was a full moon, and you're supposed to make a wish on the full moon. Mango must have gotten out while I had my eyes closed. I knew he wasn't his usual self and—"

"At least you noticed something was wrong, Zack," I interrupt. "I wasn't paying enough attention. I might have missed more than one pill. I don't even know for sure."

"A missed pill or two or ten wouldn't have made a difference," Dad says. "I promise you. I noticed a few days ago that Mango wasn't finishing his food. I know that when an animal stops showing interest in food it can mean he's preparing to go, but I honestly didn't connect the two. I wish Mango didn't have to die, but one thing I know for sure is that he didn't die to teach any of us a lesson. We all do the best we can, trying to keep all the balls in the air at once. Let's be thankful that we were able to give Mango such a wonderful life and that he gave us so much love in return." This was a long speech for my father, who is generally a man of few words.

Nobody says anything for a few minutes, and finally

Mom announces we're free to go. I drift back upstairs thinking about what my father said about keeping all the balls in the air. Deep down I know I'll always believe that I was so wrapped up in myself that I dropped the Mango ball. When I wasn't looking, the Mango ball bounced across the floor, rolled right out the back door, and settled two feet under the ground.

When I try to get out of bed Monday morning, I'm so dizzy that I have to lie back down again. My face is still swollen, and I insist that I can't possibly go to school. Mom agrees to let me stay home if I promise to eat three solid meals and take a hot shower. I agree since it's been three days since I've showered and I'm beginning to smell. At least food tastes vaguely like food now, rather than cardboard. My taste buds might be coming back, but my colors aren't. Everything is so gray and pale and lifeless now. So this is what normal feels like. That old phrase "Be careful what you wish for" seems appropriate.

The only thing that makes me feel better is watching afternoon talk shows. My life may be a mess right now, but some of these people have it worse. Maybe that's the whole appeal of talk shows in the first place.

Even though watching television helps take my mind off Mango, I'm aware that usually he would be sitting on my lap watching with me. One of the shows is on computer dating, and it reminds me of Adam. I check my e-mail and find one from Sunday night. He must have written it as soon as he got back to Boston.

DEAR MIA,

JERRY TOLD US ALL ABOUT WHAT HAPPENED TO YOUR CAT. I'M SORRY FOR YOU, BUT I THINK YOU STILL SHOULD HAVE COME TO THE MEETING. I GUESS YOU REALLY LIKE CATS. I'M ALLERGIC, SO I CAN'T SAY I LIKE THEM TOO MUCH. IT WAS NICE KISSING YOU. I HOPE WE CAN DO IT AGAIN SOMETIME. WRITE SOON, OKAY?

YOURS TRULY,
ADAM

I'm tempted to print out his letter just so I can crumple it into a tiny ball. What kind of sympathy note is that? Synesthete or not, he's pretty much a jerk. I can't believe I wasted my first kiss on him. If he hadn't kissed me and if I hadn't sat on the porch Friday night going over it in my head, Mango might not be dead right now. The thought makes my stomach cramp up.

At dinner Beth asks me, "Are you ever going to wear real clothes again? At least you're clean, finally." Then she reaches for a spring roll and asks, "There's no meat in this, right?"

Mom nods. I know she brought home Chinese food because it's my favorite.

"Hey, Mia," Zack says, carefully picking the mushrooms out of his chicken dish. "Some blond girl at school today asked me about you. Quite a babe, actually. Not as hot as your math tutor, but she still has a few years to catch up in hotness."

"Zack!" Mom scolds.

"Since when did you start liking girls anyway?" Beth asks. I was thinking the same thing. "You're only in sixth grade."

He shrugs. "Blame it on cable."

I put down my fork. "So what did this girl ask you?"

"She wanted to know if you really saw those colors in words and stuff. So I told her yeah, you do."

"That's it?"

"Yup. That's all she wrote."

"All *who* wrote?" I ask, confused.

"It's an *expression*," Zack explains impatiently. "Like 'It's not over till the fat lady sings.'"

"What fat lady?" asks Beth.

Zack sighs. "Never mind. You two don't read the right kinds of books at all. Should I not have told her anything?"

"It doesn't matter now." I don't really even care who the girl was. Now that my colors are gone, I'm sure everyone will stop paying attention to me. That's one good thing about it.

My parents refuse to hear my explanation of why I need another day at home, and come Tuesday morning, I'm forced to put on jeans and a sweater. I guess I'd make a bit of a scene if I showed up in my old flannel pajamas with the ducks on them. Jenna is already at the bus stop when Zack and I arrive. She's bouncing on her toes to keep warm. When she sees me she stops bouncing and pulls me aside.

"Hold out your arm," she demands.

I do as she asks. She pushes up the sleeve of my sweater, whips out a pair of scissors from her jacket pocket, and cuts right through my friendship bracelet. It falls to the ground, and my jaw drops open.

"Why did you do that?" I bend down to pick up the ruined bracelet. "Are you mad at me again?"

"I'm not mad at you," she says as she pulls a little white box out of her other pocket. It's the same size as the one that held my piece of the moon, and I feel a pang of regret over throwing it out the window. She opens the box to reveal a thin gold chain with a clasp. She hooks it onto my wrist and holds out her own arm to show me she's wearing the identical bracelet.

"These were my fourteenth-birthday present. From my mom," she says in a tight voice. "Her letter said she figured by now we'd be needing new ones."

The tears flow easily from both of us, and I know we're both crying for a lot of reasons.

I refuse to take the bracelet off in gym class, and the teacher tells me not to come crying to her if it breaks. As if I hadn't already cried enough for two lifetimes. In my weakened state I can barely climb the rope. The teacher tells me I can sit on the bleachers for the rest of the period. Roger gestures for me to join him on the top row. He can't climb the rope because of his ankle, but I see he had no problem climbing up the bleachers.

"So why weren't you at Jenna's party?" he asks as soon as I sit down. "I thought you guys were best friends."

"My cat died," I say bluntly, my eyes stinging at my own words. My voice sounds far away, as if it belongs to somebody else. I remember it felt that way in third grade, up at the board.

He puts his hand on my arm and leaves it there. "I'm really sorry, Mia. I didn't know."

It takes a minute for my head to stop flashing with images of the helicopter and of Mango in the ground. When I snap back to the gym, the first thing I feel is Roger's hand on my arm. I look down at it, and he quickly pulls it away.

"This might not matter much," he says quietly, "but I know how you must feel."

I open my mouth to correct him, but then I realize that he, more than anybody, *does* know how I feel. "Did it take you a long time to get over losing your dog?"

He nods. It's the first time we've acknowledged that we were both in that vet's office when his dog was put to sleep. "We had Oscar since before I was born. He was like a brother to me. I know that sounds stupid."

"No, it doesn't," I quickly assure him.

"Keeping his stuff around the house almost makes it seem like he's just in the next room, you know? Throwing it away would be like denying that he was ever there." As he's talking, Roger is forcefully twisting a loose string off his gym shorts. If he doesn't stop, his shorts might completely unravel.

I wish my father hadn't been so quick to get rid of Mango's bowls. Even Tweety's gone now. All that's really left are photographs and stray pieces of fur on my bed.

"I think we're almost ready to put the stuff away now," Roger says, giving the loose string one last firm tug. "It gets easier, Mia—missing them and feeling guilty and helpless that you couldn't save them. Oscar kind of settled into my memory, and I take him with me. Does that make sense?"

I tell him that yes, it does make sense. He smiles

and reminds me for a second of Adam. But Roger's definitely cuter. I wonder why I didn't notice it before? I'm suddenly embarrassed about how badly I behaved during our history project. I can't apologize to Mango anymore, but at least I can apologize to Roger. Before I get the chance, one of the guys in our class comes bounding up the bleachers.

"Hey, Mia, can you tell me what color my name is?"

"I don't know," I answer haltingly. "What's your name again?"

"It's Doug," he says, puffing out his chest. "As in Doug, captain of the soccer team?"

Roger rolls his eyes, and I stifle a laugh.

I concentrate for a minute. I know from memory the colors of the individual letters in his name, but I can't visualize them together to know what the word would really look like. My heart sinks. I tell him his name is hot pinkish-purple, since that's the color of the *d*.

"But that's so girly," he says, clearly disappointed.

"Sorry," I tell him. "It doesn't mean anything."

Doug shakes his head sadly and then leaps back down the bleachers, two rows at a time.

I turn back to Roger. "You know, I think you're the only person left in the school who hasn't asked me the color of their name."

He doesn't seem surprised. "Whatever color it is wouldn't matter anyway."

"What do you mean?"

"I'm color-blind," he declares.

It suddenly all makes sense, and I start laughing.

"You think it's funny that I'm color-blind?"

"No, no. It's just that—is that why your socks never used to match?"

He starts laughing too. "Yeah. I was too stubborn to let my mom pick them out for me. I got over it, though. Now she ties them together."

"We're some pair," I tell him. "You don't see enough colors, and I see too many! Well, I used to anyway. Now they're gone."

His eyes widen in surprise. "Will they come back?"

I tell him I don't know as the teacher blows the whistle for us to go to the locker rooms. Roger and I stand up, and before we head off in different directions, he says, "You're right about one thing."

"What's that?"

"We're some pair." He turns away before I can see his face and hobbles down the bleachers. I watch him go. For that brief moment my heart lifts and I almost feel happy. But then Mango's little furry face appears in my head, and it hits me like a punch in the stomach that he won't be waiting on my bed for me when I get home today.

After school I ask the secretary in the main office if anyone in the school has the last name Henkle. She says there's a Hansly and an O'Henry, but no Henkle. I'm not sure anymore why I want to find Billy. Am I hoping I can help him or that he can help me?

I make it through the week with recurring pangs of pain and loss and guilt, and after dinner on Friday night I put on the pajamas that I plan to stay in for the rest of the weekend. Jenna has invited me to stay over her house, but I'm just not ready to have fun yet. Today was the first morning that Mango's death didn't crush me the second I opened my eyes. It actually waited until I had turned off the alarm and pushed down my covers. Dad said that any progress is a good thing, but I still don't see the purple spirals that I used to see when my alarm went off. I admit it—I miss those purple spirals. And I haven't been able to go into the backyard since Mango's funeral.

The phone rings around seven o'clock, and my dad tells me to pick it up in the living room. It's Jerry, calling from his lab.

"You hanging in there?" he asks. It's good to hear his voice.

"I guess so," I tell him, plopping down in my dad's

new reclining chair. It was a birthday present from Mom.

"You're a strong girl, Mia. You'll get through this."

"If I'm so strong, then why are all my colors gone?"

He doesn't answer right away. "When did that happen?"

"Right after Mango...after he...after he died."

"How do you feel about it?"

"Empty," I tell him honestly. "Flat."

"That's normal," he assures me. I'm having a hard time getting used to people calling my actions *normal*. "Your colors will return, Mia. I promise. And you'll feel three-dimensional again. Try doing something creative to jump-start your brain a little. You told me you like to paint; why don't you try that?"

I agree to try, even though I haven't been able to even look at my paints lately. After we hang up I go back to my room and stare at my easel. There's a thin layer of dust on it. I'm still torn between wanting my colors back and feeling like it's an appropriate punishment that they're gone. I decide to leave it up to fate. If they come back, it won't be because of anything I actively do. I pick up the wooden easel with one hand, fold up the legs, and bring it over to my closet. I have to push aside a lot of junk to make room for it, and I suddenly find myself staring at the painting I did of Grandpa. I hadn't given it much thought after the rain ruined it. I reach in, carefully pull it out, and lean it up against my wall.

Something is different. I kneel down to look closer. I distinctly remember when I finished painting it that Grandpa had a faraway look in his eyes. But now he looks almost content. I definitely don't remember painting him that way. I feel a stab in my heart when I look on Grandpa's shoulder and see the gray smudge that was once Mango. Then my heart starts beating faster as I notice paw prints on the painting from where Mango walked across it. The paw prints lead right off the top of the canvas and, I imagine, straight up to heaven. I don't think I need to offer him there myself anymore; I think Grandpa did it for me. Maybe Mango was Grandpa's parting gift to me, and now they're in heaven together with Grams. I really, truly want to believe that.

I wrestle a frame off another old painting from the back of my closet and put the blurred portrait in it. I hang it in the center of the wall, opposite all my clocks, so it will be the last thing I see when I go to bed and the first thing I see when I wake up.

The doorbell rings early Saturday morning, and I roll over in bed, certain that it's not for me. But two minutes later my mother comes in and tells me to get dressed because I have company.

"Is it Jenna?" I ask, pushing myself up on my elbows.

"No. Believe it or not, it's that woman I met at the supermarket at the end of the summer. Remember? You were talking to her little boy. Their last name's Henkle, I think."

I throw off my covers and race across the room to my dresser. My clothes from yesterday are conveniently still crumpled on my chair, and I quickly pull them on.

"I guess you do remember," my mother says, picking up the pajamas I left in the middle of the floor.

"How did they find us?" I ask breathlessly.

"Her daughter goes to your school. Judging from how Zack's fawning over her, I think this is the 'babe' he was talking about at dinner the other night."

I grab a ponytail holder from my night-table drawer and tie back my hair. A minute later I'm standing in the living room. Billy jumps out of the recliner and gives me a big hug while his mother watches from the couch. She looks slightly embarrassed—maybe because the last time we saw each other she was rude to me in the elementary-school gym.

"I'm sorry to barge in on you like this," she says, glancing from me to my mother and back to me. "But we were in the neighborhood and...well, Billy seems to have this attachment to you, and I thought maybe you could help us."

Just then the "babe" walks out of the kitchen, with Zack trailing right behind her. She's holding a big glass of orange juice, and Zack looks proud, as if he squeezed it himself. She stops when she sees me, causing Zack to bump right into her. I don't think he minded.

"This is my daughter, Amy," Mrs. Henkle says.

My first thought is the rhyme from my morbid poster. A *is for Amy who fell down the stairs*. My second thought is that I know her. She's the girl who was so obnoxious to me in the cafeteria when people first found out about my colors. She said I'd wind up in a special class. Instead I wound up hiding in a bathroom stall because of her.

"We've met," I say stiffly. "But wait a second. I checked if anyone at school had Billy's last name and no one did."

"Amy still uses my ex-husband's name," Mrs. Henkle explains.

Amy's cheeks flush pink as she turns toward me. "I'm, uh, sorry about, well, you know," she says.

"It's okay," I mutter, without really meaning it.

Billy wraps his arms around my leg as Mrs. Henkle

pushes herself up from the couch. "Amy told me that letters and numbers have color for you," she says to me. "And I realize you were trying to tell me about it a few weeks ago. Ever since Billy met you, this color thing is all he talks about."

Billy nods happily, and I smile at him. Smiling is starting to feel less foreign.

"So what do you think I should do?" she asks, sounding helpless. "His kindergarten teacher is talking about putting him in a special class next year because of this."

I glance at Amy, who looks away. "There's nothing wrong with Billy," I tell Mrs. Henkle. "I've met other people who have synesthesia—that's what it's called—and they're totally fine."

Billy is busy fidgeting with the lever that turns the chair into a recliner. I don't know how much of this conversation he understands, but I think on some level he's aware that this is a turning point for him.

Mrs. Henkle is still not convinced. "But isn't there anything to treat this...this...disease?"

Zack steps forward before I can respond. His eyes are blazing. "My sister doesn't have a disease. She has a gift."

I gape at him gratefully as he steps back next to Amy, who has a new look of respect in her eyes. I don't think many people stand up to her mother.

"What color is my name, Mia?" Billy asks gleefully, breaking the moment of silence.

"Your name is light brown like wood, with some sky blue sprinkled in," I reply, kneeling next to him. "And it's sort of mushy."

"Like oatmeal?" he asks hopefully.

"Just like oatmeal."

"No, it's not," he says, laughing and bouncing in his seat. "It's bright pink and shiny like my granddaddy's head!"

"Um, Mia," my mother says. "Does this mean your colors are back?"

I stand up with a start. The words in my head are in color again, and I didn't even notice it. I excuse myself and run upstairs to check out my alphabet poster. Good ol' sunflower-yellow *a*. Shimmering green *j*. Robin's-egg-blue *z*. They're all back. The experience feels so familiar and so foreign at the same time. I think it's because so much has changed. I have no idea how to be this new person. I head back downstairs.

"Thank you for your time," Mrs. Henkle says to my mom and me as she hands Billy his jacket. "You've given me a lot to think about. Amy is cheering at a school basketball game, so we have to go now."

Zack looks stricken. "But Amy said she wanted to see my McDonald's chart. It'll only take a minute."

"I'll be right back, Mom," Amy says. Zack beams as if he can't believe his luck and leads her upstairs. I guess she isn't all that bad. While they're upstairs Mom writes out Jerry's phone number at the university for Mrs. Henkle. Billy hugs me good-bye, and I promise him we'll keep in touch. Amy comes back down and says, "You and your friends should come to one of the games sometime. They're fun."

"Maybe we will," I say, closing the door behind her. Jenna might take some convincing, but she'd probably do it. I wonder if Roger likes sports? I offer to help my mother make breakfast, and she eagerly accepts.

"I'm proud of you, Mia," my mother says, carefully pouring the pancake batter into a large glass bowl.

I toss some frozen blueberries into the mix. "Why?"

"That was a great thing you did, with Billy. You gave him the head start we weren't able to give you." She's stirring the pancake mixture so fast that I'm sure it's about to fly out of the bowl.

"Mom, don't feel bad," I tell her, steadying the bowl with my hand. "You and Dad didn't know what was going on."

She rests the spoon on a piece of paper towel. "That's not entirely true."

"Huh?" I drop the blueberry I was about to pop in my mouth.

My mother quickly scoops up the blueberry before it has a chance to stain the wooden countertop. She throws it in the sink and then starts scrubbing the counter without looking me in the eye. "The night you told us about your problems at school, I couldn't sleep. Something was nagging at me. Finally, last week, it hit me."

I wait expectantly for her to continue.

"You don't remember Grams too well, do you?" she asks, finally looking straight at me.

I shake my head, wondering what Grams could have to do with anything. "I remember her dancing in the living room with Grandpa a lot. I remember she was always playing records on Dad's old stereo."

"Yes, she loved music," my mother says. "Last week I was in the car, and one of her favorite old songs came on the radio. I suddenly remembered her telling me that she loved music so much because she could see the colors in the air all around her."

"Are you serious?" I ask in disbelief.

"I thought she was just being imaginative. I didn't know she meant it *literally*. Then one day I saw you dancing in the living room with her. You couldn't have been more than two and a half years old, but the two of you were having a grand time. I heard her say, 'Aren't the colors beautiful?' and you said, in your little-girl voice, 'Yes, Grams, they're bootiful.' But I still didn't think anything of it, Mia. I'm so sorry. I should have taken it more seriously."

"I don't remember that at all," I say sadly. I wonder how different things would have been if Grams hadn't died when I was so young. "And Dad never heard her mention anything when he was growing up?"

Mom shakes her head. "I asked him as soon as I recalled the incident. He said that his mother had always been very quiet. Apparently your grandpa did enough talking for both of them."

I smile, remembering how Grandpa's deep voice could be heard from every corner of the house. I bet my whole life would have been different if Grams had stuck around. As I watch my mother pour the batter onto the frying pan, it hits me that if Grandpa knew about Grams's colors—which he *must* have after being married to her for forty years—then maybe he knew about mine too. I can't believe I threw away his gift. I leave my mother to her pancake flipping, slip on my boots and coat, and head out the front door. I look up at my bedroom window and then position myself underneath it. Grandpa's moon piece should have landed right around here, but the ground is so wet and muddy that I can't find it. It must have disintegrated by now and become part of the grass. I finally give up the search, resigned to the fact that the gift is lost forever.

"Are you all right?" my dad asks as I kick off my boots.

"I just keep doing stupid things," I tell him. "Things I wind up regretting."

He takes off my coat and hangs it up. "Welcome to being human. It's part of the package."

"Not for me," Zack announces as he bounds down the stairs in his socks and slides up to us. "I intend to overcome my humanness. I will become a god."

"What kind of god will you be?" I ask.

Trying unsuccessfully to pat down his messy hair, he says, "I'm still working on that part. But I will make the world a better place. Somehow or other."

"That sounds very noble, Zack," Dad says.

"Oh, and I'll wear a really awesome outfit," Zack adds. "With a cape."

"You'll be a big hit next Halloween," I tell him. "At least you can finally throw out those Spock ears."

"Who?" Zack asks innocently.

"Exactly."

"Looks like our family's back to normal," Dad says to Mom as we sit down for breakfast.

I drop my fork, and it clanks loudly against my plate. "How can you say that?" Everyone stops eating.

"Grandpa's not here anymore. Mango's not here anymore. How is this normal?"

"Mia," Dad says calmly, "change is normal."

"Then I don't *want* to be normal."

"Uh, Mia," Zack says, "I don't think you need to worry about that."

I'm so tired of my emotions flipping back and forth. I don't think I'm handling change very well at all.

With his mouth full of pancakes, Dad asks, "Is it true that your colors are back? That must make you happy."

I nod. "It does, it's just that..." I don't know how to tell them that while I'm very grateful, I still feel guilty. Like I don't deserve something special.

"Oh, I almost forgot!" Mom says, smacking the side of her head. "We're invited to the Roths' this evening for the first night of Hanukkah."

"I have a date," Beth announces.

"With Brent?" I ask, not really expecting a response.

She surprises me by saying yes.

Mom tells her she can meet her date afterward, and Beth pouts.

"I don't really feel up to going," I tell her.

"We're all going," my mother says firmly. "It will be good for us to do something as a family again."

Dad puts down his glass. "But tonight's my poker night, I can't—"

"We're all going," my mother insists, using her non-negotiable tone. "The whole neighborhood will be there. One more word out of any of you and we're not getting a Christmas tree this year."

Beth stands up and puts her plate in the sink. "Do you have any idea how many trees are cut down each year just so we can hang pretty lights on them?"

My mother pushes her plate to the side and lays her head down on the table. I know how she feels.

Six hours later we're in the Roths' living room watching their twin sons play a game with a wooden top called a dreidel. They always ask us to play, but we can never figure out the rules. Sometimes I think the boys switch places in the middle of the game just to mix us up. The doorbell rings, and Jenna and her dad come in, followed by an older couple who have recently moved in next door to the Roths.

Jenna and I go to the back of the room to talk. "I miss you," she says. "It's been forever since we've hung out together."

"I miss you too," I tell her and mean it.

"I've been working on a great PIC mission," she whispers. "You know, when you feel up to it."

"Can you give me a hint?"

"Let's just say it'll be our biggest job ever." She tries to wink, but it looks more like she's got something in her eye.

The Roths always let each of the kids light a candle on the menorah, and when it's my turn, I say a prayer in my head for Grams and Grandpa and Mango. I tell them I'm sorry our time together on this earth was so short and that I miss them. When Zack's turn arrives he looks up at Mom for permission. He's still banned from anything to do with fire. Mom nods her head slightly, and Zack lights his candle without burning anything. Afterward, Mrs. Roth busies herself by making sure the wax doesn't drip all over the glass table, while everyone else gathers in the dining room for dessert. Out of the corner of my eye I see Zack sneak out of the room, unnoticed by everyone except me. A minute later he runs back in and frantically waves me over.

"What is it?" I hiss. "You can't just go snooping around people's houses."

He drags me out of the room and down the hall. "Trust me, you'll want to see this."

"Anything that starts with you saying 'trust me' makes me instantly suspicious."

"Look!" he says, and points into the den. A low wooden gate keeps us from entering. In the corner of the room, on top of a big pillow, is the Roths' cat Twinkles. Curled up around her belly are five tiny kittens. "Look at that one by her leg," he says, pointing to the smallest kitten.

I put my hand over my mouth.

"It looks just like Mango, doesn't it?" he says. "When he was a baby."

I nod, unable to take my eyes away from the tiny thing.

"I guess we know who the father was!" Zack says, laughing. "That Mango always was a lady's man. Er, a lady's cat. I mean, a lady cat's cat, or no, I mean—"

"It's okay, Zack. I get it. I wish Mango were around to see this."

"Maybe he's watching right now," Zack says. "I bet he's an angel cat."

"So you found our kittens, eh?" Mr. Roth appears beside us and we jump. He doesn't seem angry at all. "They're not ready to leave their mother yet, but in about a month we'll be looking for homes for them. Let us know if you're interested."

"We want one," Zack says, his eyes shining. "The littlest one."

I whirl around to face Zack. "What? No, we don't. Sorry, Mr. Roth, just ignore him."

"Well, let me know if you change your mind," Mr. Roth says, leaving us alone.

"Why'd you say that, Mia? I want him."

"How can you think of replacing Mango already?"

"It's *Mango's son*. Or daughter. It's not just any cat."

"Zack, if Mango was the father, then they're *all* his children. How could we just take *one?*"

"I hadn't thought of that," he admits. "Hmm..." he says, and walks slowly back to the living room, no doubt hatching some plan to get Mom and Dad to take all of them. That will never happen.

I glance behind me and then climb easily over the gate. Twinkles looks up at me warily and keeps an eye on me as I approach. I bend over to get a better look at the kittens. It's uncanny how much the littlest one looks like Mango. My eyes cloud up, and I have to lean my head back for a few seconds to avoid letting the tears slip out. I reach out my hand and lightly pet his little head. He opens his squinty eyes and yawns. Then he lets out a surprisingly strong mustard-colored meow and settles back into his mother's warmth. Who ever heard of a cat named Mustard? Impossible.

That night Dad knocks on my door as I'm about to switch off my lamp.

"Come in," I say, leaning up in bed.

He walks in and sits on the edge of the bed. "I thought you'd want to have this." He hands me Mango's Winnie-the-Pooh blanket. I sit all the way up and rub the familiar material between my fingers. Some stray Mango fur is embedded in it. I never thought I'd see it again.

"But I thought you buried Mang...I mean, that Mango was bur...I mean...oh, I can't even say the words."

"I saved it for you. I thought you might want it back."

I look at him gratefully and hold the blanket up to my nose. "It still smells like him." A mixture of cat food, the outdoors, and litter.

"He loved sleeping on that blanket," Dad says on his way out of my room. I hug the blanket to my chest and then sniff it a few more times before laying it at the foot of the bed where it belongs.

That night I dream I'm at the county fair with Zack. We're eating hot dogs with gobs of mustard and laughing at Beth, who's stuck on top of the Ferris wheel.

When I wake up I swear I can still smell mustard. It doesn't take me too long to figure out what the dream means.

Although Web sites are always changing, an online search for synesthesia (also spelled synaesthesia) will lead you to a wealth of information. You can also refer to *The Man Who Tasted Shapes* by Dr. Richard E. Cytowic and *Synaesthesia: Classic and Contemporary Readings*, edited by Simon Baron-Cohen and John E. Harrison.

Two places to find help dealing with the death of a pet are the Association for Pet Loss and Bereavement (*http://www.aplb.org*) and the Pet Loss Support Page (*http://www.pet-loss.net*). These two Web sites offer local support centers, counselors, hot lines, and more. A selection of books to guide readers through the grieving process include *The Loss of a Pet* by Wallace Sife and *When Your Pet Dies: How to Cope with Your Feelings* by Jamie Quackenbush and Denise Graveline. For younger readers, try Dr. Diane Pomerance's *When Your Pet Dies*, Christine Davis's *For Every Cat an Angel* and *For Every Dog an Angel*, Cynthia Rylant's *Dog Heaven* and *Cat Heaven*, and Judith Viorst's *The Tenth Good Thing about Barney*. To adopt a pet from a local shelter, visit Petfinder.com.

Acknowledgments

I owe a debt of gratitude to my agent, Ginger Knowlton, for her unflagging faith; my esteemed editor, Maria Modugno, for embracing *Mango* and giving the book such a wonderful home; and to Sean Day and the synesthetes on his Internet list who so generously shared their stories and answered my questions. I am also truly grateful to my early readers for their insights and patience: Laura Hoffman, Stuart P. Levine, Hayley Mitchell Haugen, Martin Lowenstein, Allison M. Dickson, Jennifer Mass, William Siedler, Michele Wells, Justin Conforti, Stacey Lowenstein, Linda Raedisch, Janel Rodriguez, and Niki Parella. You guys are cooler than Buffy. Okay, almost.

A special thank you to Judy Blume and Karen Cushman for being so supportive, warm, and inspiring. It's been a great gift.

1. Mia finds her cat, Mango, near her grandfather's grave shortly after his death. How does Mango help Mia deal with her grief? Why do you think she says that part of her grandfather's soul is in Mango?

2. Have you ever had an adult or friend not believe you when you tried to tell them something important? How do you think the incident in the classroom (when Mia was eight) affected her?

3. Mia uses her ability to see numbers as colors to help her cheat on a math quiz. Do you think she is wrong to do this? Do you think Mia is taking the easy way out by using her colors? Why or why not?

4. When Mia's parents finally believe Mia and decide to take her to the doctor, she struggles with whether or not she wants to be "cured" of seeing colors. Have you ever had to choose between keeping something

that makes you special and giving it up to fit in with everyone else? If so, what did you decide and why?

5. After Mia loses Mango, she realizes that she has also lost her colors. Jerry had warned her that synesthesia can be affected by traumatic events. How does this loss help Mia realize how important her synesthesia is to her?

6. Mia's relationships with her family and friends are greatly affected when they learn about her synesthesia. Track the development of her relationships with her family members and with Jenna and Roger. How would you react if one of your friends told you he or she has synesthesia?

7. Do you have synesthesia? Do you wish you did? Why or why not?

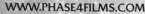